Just
for your
Smile

BAMAN TADIWALA

Dedication

Mummy-Daddy, Mumma-Papa
&
To all people who bring positive vibes to this writer.

About the Author

I know you and your mobile phone are inseparable. So why don't you try your luck by scanning these QR codes? Let's begin with the one on top followed by the remaining three.

P.S. Be My Angel
(2015)

An Imperfect Book
(2018)

A Two Page Story
(2019)

PROLOGUE

March 15, 2007

You're the best in the world,' she said as she placed the half-eaten piece of Paratha in his mouth. He was still doing—last minute revision, for one of the most dangerous exams of India—IIT JEE .

Harshil, time's up!' she said, and checked if he had taken his hall ticket and the other accessories.

Dhak… Dhak… Dhak…

Such was his position—like every brat, who marched out that day—to chunk the three hour long exam. These three hours were the sole barrier between him, and his dream—IIT. He held the hall ticket in his fists and touched his Mother's feet to seek her blessings. She caressed his temple and hugged him.

Her blessings were everything to him. She was not simply his Mother, but the solitary love till date in his life. After commending him, she took him inside his Father's bedroom and said, Bless our son. It's an important day for him.'

There was no response from his side. Mom, why do you do this?' She was cut short. Harshil didn't reply further and quietly passed out knowing what would follow thereafter. He had seen that for years now.

On looking back, he knew she was glaring at her man's memory on the wall. Fifteen years had flown by, but every single day turned out to be the same for her.

Harshil stepped out of his house like a brave warrior. He thought about this exam as a battle royal, and he was a warrior—fighting for the tears of his Mother. She had a dream to see him study at IIT.

Hope can make an individual weak, but her confidence had led him to a purpose in his life. Trust affirms the reality, but her duty towards him had become an inspiration for him.

Sometimes to fill his belly, she starved empty. So today, Harshil had an opportunity to do something for her, and set forth, it was meant — just for your smile.

#INCOMPLETE_HARSHIL

After ten years…
15 February 2017

Do media have any sympathy when they annoy the well-known personalities by asking personal questions? There was this reporter — Amayraj Singh, who followed Harshil since the day one of his corporate success.

Initially, Harshil entertained him, as the pumps were relevant, and they were stationed on his work. But gradually, Amayraj began to ask something about the word Love' and linked its affiliation to Harshil's life. As a cause, Harshil avoided Amayraj on most of the occasions.

When you avoid someone, it either produces the distance or animosity

Due to Harshil's ignorance, Amayraj felt offended. That insult resulted into anger. Anger ignited ego, and that ego gave rise to one story in Amayraj's mind. He wrote a fictitious love story out of Harshil and especially termed him as — Incomplete.

What was worse? That story became the new gossip topic for media. TV channels earned TRP's. All leading newspapers, magazines printed that crap.

On noticing that shit being published under his name, Harshil got furious. He held his temperament because he knew further comments would give birth to a new storyline for the media. Everyone possesses a breaking point and Harshil was no new.

One day when Amayraj wrote something more about him, a hash tag under the name of —#IncompleteHarshil‖ began to trend on twitter. And it was sufficient to break his submission

Bunny, organize a press conference,' he said. 'Today, I'll dismiss all the confusions,'

Harshil, your one statement can set up an extensive drama all over the state,'

Let that happen. Enough is enough. I'm done with my patience.'

I will not call Amayraj. He is the most irritating journalist I've ever come across. If we invite him, he will unquestionably create one more controversy under your name,'

He thinks he's the boss of the media, but now, I need to teach him his actual foundations.'

What will you tell him?'

The truth,'

Have you lost it? If you say the truth, these people won't spare you,'

That is where you are again mistaken. You can't kill someone who is already dead from inside.' Bunny didn't utter a single word after that remark from Harshil.

—You can't kill someone who is already dead from inside.‖—This one statement from Harshil was a claim to all the misfortunes he had been through in his past. Perhaps he was still going through!

Harshil was successful, but only Bunny knew the reason of why had Harshil given up living for himself after the incident that completely transformed his life.

HOW COULD I FORGET THAT DAY?

When Harshil saw Amayraj, he was receptive of that cunning look, and his witty brain, which was full of irrelevant questions.

So let's start the press conference,' said the coordinator.

No wait!' Harshil interrupted.

What happened, sir?' commented Amayraj, who was sitting in the front of him.

Harshil avoided. Oh, I see. It's the fear of dealing with my interrogations, isn't it?' asked Amayraj

Harshil abstained from defending those provoking remarks.

Deep inside, the anger was so strained, but every single time when he looked into Amayraj's eyes, that angry would sink down on its very own.

Harshil knew Amayraj was cunning. His eyes depicted that cunningness, but those eyes still had the magic to clutch everyone's attention—such was his personality!

Finally, Harshil looked at him and answered, No, Amayraj. I'm not afraid of facing your questions. All I desire is the recording of this press conference shouldn't be aired live,'

Why? This indubitably shows your suspicion to wrestle with tough and personal questions,'

It's not so, Amayraj. Our company respects media.

We tolerate each and every ass of media. Well, that involves you as well.'

Sometimes, we guys also have to tolerate personalities like you. Not a great deal!'

Who is telling you to tolerate me?' Harshil questioned.

Leave it, sir! Else people will declare that you termed media as an intolerant,'

I'm doing my job, and if you ask any question pertained to my work, I will cheerfully answer it. But who offered you the right to produce a story out of my personal life?'

Some columnists and reporters who were initially showing their anger towards Harshil went dumb for three or four minutes, but not Amayraj!

Harshil looked at everyone and declared, But now you can ask me anything. I can't bear the wrong wimps which are been circulated under my name.'

Amayraj took hold and asked, In one of your interviews, you mentioned you've seen GOD. How is that possible?'

Yes, that's true,'

But how?'

I see God everywhere. Even in you, Amayraj. Difference is, you're the only one against me,'

I'm not against you. My journalism has taught me to be fair in every matter. So, on your petition, I'm not broadcasting this press conference live, but in exchange, I want to know one thing,'

And what is that?'

Your real life love story.'

Bunny, Harshil's only best ally, and the CEO of the

company interrupted Amayraj and said, Are you crazy? Do you've any idea to whom you're talking to?'

Amayraj laughed and said, I'm taking to someone who is still trending on Twitter as an incomplete,'

Bh******!! Stop teasing him, or else I'll accuse you if you further blabber anything,' Bunny said, hot blooded.

Bunny openly enraged Amayraj.

You are an idiot! You abused me, Bho******? Go on and sue me. I'm an independent person. Instead, I should sue you, Mr. Bunny. How could a person like you, with no proper degree, become the CEO of such a big company?'

The press conference was going into the deep argument. The other reporters, who were sitting patiently, verbally abused Bunny.

Harshil got up from his place and yelled in a harsh tone, Stop. Enough! You want your answer, Amayraj? Guess what? You got it!'

Harshil started to tremble. On observing that, Bunny approached him and said, Say nothing. Please! Let them abuse me.'

How long we will wrap it? You know it's not our company, and you also know for whom we are working since last seven years.'

Harshil then looked at Amayraj and said, Love — the only word which you think that is lacking from my life. Life seems fucking odd when you have lots of money, but still you remain apart. Life seems fucking boring when you can manage to go to expensive restaurants, but alone. Life seems fucking hard, when you have expensive cell phone like i-phone 6s, but you don't get a single text from any girl. Loneliness kills, and to add more suffering to it, emptiness kills more. I'm also the victim of such a thing.'

He further said, Yes, the only tonic missing from my live is — LOVE! Bunny never had a girlfriend. He always had girlfriends. I also wanted a girlfriend, but I never got one.'

And why is that?' asked Amayraj.

Reason number one: I was not an advancing personality. Reason number two: I never understood how to communicate with any girl. Reason number three: I couldn't see into the eyes of any girl. Reason number four and possibly the most remarkable one: I never knew how to carry on the conversation after the word — okay.'

So these remain the four major reasons you're single till date?' Amayraj asked.

Not till the day she visited my house. How could I forget that day? Every bite of that day makes me remember her presence….'

MOTHER,
PLEASE DON'T FETCH A GIRL FOR ME

Before seven years, 2010

How would you deal with arranged marriages in India? First of all, like a social survey, you would survey about the two families. After the survey has satisfactory reports, you would approach the common links of that family, and find out if the family background is acceptable or not.

If that stage is also cleared, then just like sending a friend request on Facebook, you would send a proposal of fixing a casual meeting between the two families. And in this entire process what does a guy and a girl get?

Absolutely nothing, expect the ugly and the embarrassing staring which both of they share while their families are conversing.

Harshil had determined not to rise early that day. He certainly wanted to ward off all those scenes.

Harshil....' she screamed vociferously. Have you lost it? Today they are coming to see you, but you're still snoring. Get up!'

After marriage, Harshil's better-half would suck his blood, and before that, those conventions were carried off by his Mother.

However, Harshil didn't give a heave to what she said, and once again dragged the blanket and went asleep.

Harshil...' she screamed again.

What is wrong with you, mom? It's barely seven in the morning. Let me sleep for some time more,'

At least today you should have been ready early,'

When are they coming?' he asked, rubbing his eyes. Seven in the evening,'

Oh come on, Mom. Let me sleep then...' he declared and hit his head on the cozy pillow.

She tugged off his blanket and tossed it on the floor.

Enough! Now straighten up and get ready. You don't even have appropriate clothes to wear. How will you face them?'

It's literally a great part. It will dispose of the actual impression that we belong to a middle class family,' he said.

Her facial expressions resolved in flashes as soon as she listened to that statement. Harshil got hold of her palm and told, Is there any necessity to look artificial? If that we are small, then we are!'

Your marriage is very important thing for our family, and for that I'm willing to do everything. I will dress up like a prima donna, and you shall look like a prince. Such occasions don't happen frequently in our lives. So what's bad if we grow little artificial to look quite sophisticated and decent?' she emphasized.

Harshil kissed her fists and said, That's why you're the best Mother in this world. But are you sure the girl will like me? And also will I like her?'

She is beautiful, and I've said this many times,' she said.

The last time when we discussed about her, I didn't even ask for her photo. Show me her photo, please!'

No Harshil, but rest assured — I'm your Mother, and every Mother fetches a beautiful and elegant girl for his son. Every Mother can judge a girl — just from her photo, and trust me, this girl is perfect for you. After me, she is the one who will keep you happy,' she said.

Hey! You're not going away from me,' he said. Little emotionally.

I'm now tired. Ask me, how tough it was to nurture you without the support of your father. We were left with handful of money. Sometimes I had to stay hungry — just to make you efficient, and you proved yourself.'

She added, You never washed away my sacrifices. You studied well and got a good job. So now it's the perfect time to build your own family.' she said.

Not my family, Mom. It will be our family!'

She chuckled and asked, If someday you buy a big house, then will you keep your old Mother there?'

Keep — is an improper word. I will stay with my old Mother in that house,' he answered.

That's my boy!' she exclaimed, and clasped him

tight. Before you meet them, I want to tell you one important thing.'

And what is that?'

She is a girl. Just as you long for me, she yearns for her parents. Just like I'm special for you, they might be special for her. So today, when they come, please don't mess up and behave nicely. I've said this because I realize what's cooking in your brain!' she said.

I'll try,' he responded.

She handed over his wallet and said, I've put some money in your wallet. Go and purchase brand new cloths for yourself,' she said.

Please haan… This shopping and all, I can't do,' Harshil said in anxiety.

So you're not going?'

No,'

Don't worry aunty, I'll take him.' remarked one familiar voice from behind.

Both of them were surprised as well as amused to see him. He was Bunny, Harshil's only best friend.

Oye…What are you doing here?' Harshil asked him.

Bunny looked at Harshil's Mother and said, A girl is coming to see him, and this fool didn't even say a single word.'

Bunny, now it's your responsibility to make him well-proportioned till evening,' she said and dusted the furniture.

Bunny gave him that sweet angry look and said, 16 GB's in laptop, 8 GB's in pen drive, 2.5 GB's in memory card, and rest 20 GB's in computer. Such was the collection I had given you, but you still want to get married?'

It's monotonous to hear your favourite one every day,'

Take her name with little respect. Mia is the only hope for the guys like me,' Bunny said aloud.

To his bad luck, Harshil's Mother learned this thing and came flying.

Yes, yes. I've learned this name somewhere,' she said.

Harshil showed an eye to Bunny and singled him to answer his mother about Mia.

Bunny was bold enough. He said, Aunty, she is a po….,'

Harshil immediately interrupted Bunny and said, He means to say that she is a pop star.'

Before she could question further, Harshil took Bunny inside his room and said, You almost killed me today. Why are you obsessed so much with porn?'

Why? Don't you love it?'

Yaar Bunny, I can't take this Chutiyapa of porn every day. It only satisfied for a few days,'

Is your organ working?' Bunny asked him with a suspicion.

It's working, and much better than yours,'

Oh! So you've tested my organ as well?'

I'm glad you didn't say I've tasted,' Harshil replied.

Shut up, or else I will cut it off,' Bunny said in anger.

I don't trust you, you can do anything,' said Harshil, circling his knuckles over his manhood.

Enough! But this is just not fair!' Bunny said.

What?'

I understand that in college you wanted to study, so you didn't even look at any girl.'

That's right.'

You pledged me that after graduation, you will have dollies around you. Where were those dollies, bro?

Your all personal desires come to a stop when you have to grapple someone's expectation. I was expected to earn from the very next day after the graduation. So yes, I didn't see the point for all that,' Harshil said.

Are you happy with your job?' Bunny asked.

I'm doing my duty with full interest, and I believe that I'll be promoted soon,' Harshil said as they took off their journey for buying liveries for the evening.

Bunny sat at the driver's seat and said, I'm thrilled for you. At least now you'll have a girl in your life. I was incessantly bothered about your hand.'

My hand? Why?'

Now your hand shall get relief,'

Go to hell, Bunny. These HD movies have made you sick.'

After few moments, Harshil suddenly revealed, I knew nothing! I was very confused with my life. I wanted to make money. I wished for a good house, but never dreamed about any girl. But deep inside, I also wanted to go through that fire which you and other guys in the college faced during the relationship.'

What type of relationship you would have preferred?' Bunny asked.

Options? That also in relationships? That's queer!' Harshil exclaimed.

That's the biggest play of the relationships, beta! If you had wished for a relationship you had to choose between a short-term or long-term relationship.'

Are you selling condoms?' Harshil

asked Fuck no! What are you saying?'

What are you saying? How can any relationship be of a short or long-term?' Harshil argued.

Nothing in this world is perpetual, particularly relationships. There exist barely any relationships that last forever. So it's worth it you weren't engaged into all that,' Bunny said.

I always longed for a relationship that would last till my last puff,'

That was tough to find in the college.'

Who even cared? I was willing to wait.' Harshil said.

You never felt lonely?' Bunny asked.

Being single doesn't point to loneliness. It's just one simple message for my future wife,'

What is that message?'

I'll just tell her, I was never made for someone because I was making myself efficient for her.'

You are still the same!' Bunny said patting Harshil's back.

A person who changes with the time is probably a wise human, but a person who even doesn't change with the time is a true friend.

Time had changed both of them. Distance had stood between them, but they never changed for each other. Their friendship always continued the same. Harshil believed only one good thing had taken place so far, and that was being given a partner like Bunny in his life.

Don't fail to remember me after you have your girl.' Bunny said.

Look, who's saying this?'

A MILLION DOLLER GIRL

Everything was set as they were waiting the Girl's arrival. However, Harshil felt nervous and uncomfortable. Nervous because he was unknown of how people talked during the sessions of arranged marriages. And uncomfortable because the outfit, Bunny had forcefully chosen for him was tight in fitting.

I told you this outfit won't suit me, but you...' Harshil said.

Ghanta!' Bunny responded with a mischievous grin on his face.

Look, they have arrived.' shouted Harshil's Mother from the kitchen.

As soon as she said that, Harshil desperately glanced outside the window. At the first sight itself, the family showed that they were rich enough.

Wow! Your future father-in-law seems rich, dude! BMW sports car.' Bunny commented.

Harshil laughed and said, This marriage will never take place,'

Why?'

They have arrived in BMW, and now you guess their expectations from me!'

The lady from the kitchen came in the hall and said, Oh idiots! Why are you standing here? Receive them.'

That was the ultimate duty left to be done,' Harshil taunted his mother.

Both of them went outside and directed the driver to park the car.

First person to show up from the BMW was the Girl's Father, Mr. Harijit Sahani. Harshil went near him, and sought a casual handshake and added, Welcome uncle...'

Mr. Sahani developed a sheepish smile on his face and gaily greeted him, Harshil, is that you?'

Yes uncle,' Harshil replied.

Bunny silently groaned, As you instructed the driver to park the car, the man must have felt you're the watchman of this house.'

Next person to step out from the BMW was the Girl's Mother, Mrs. Simran Sahani. Both Harshil and Bunny traditionally greeted her by saying—Namaste! This kind and disciplined gesture brought forth a smirk on her fat face.

Having received both of them, Harshil's Mother inquired, Where is our Girl, Mr. Sahani?'

What do I tell, Mrs. Rama? She is a rather fair adolescent. She informed us she would not travel in our BMW,'

In a fraction of subordinates, black Royal Enfield bike with maximum speed dashed inside the gateway.

There she is, our daughter, Manshita,' remarked Mrs. Sahani

Harshil was tantalized on seeing her perfectly curved physique in those black bikers outfit.

Shimmering mercury aviators on the pearly white face, dark red lipstick, and a nose ring was adequate to personify her temperature.

She turned off the engine.

Damn!' exclaimed Bunny on observing that seducing side glace she produced as she rested the bike on its side stand.

Both the Sahani couple and Harshil's Mother felt little embarrassed. But the men in blue were enjoying the sight of the lady in black.

As Manshita approached further, Harshil could clearly have a first peek of her face.

Why does an every ordinary eye look extraordinary when eyeliner is applied to it?' he asked himself

Those attractive dark eyes doubled the charm of her face.

Mr. Sahani looked at Manshita and asked, Now what is this?'

Sorry Dad. Today itself I got this bike from Viveek. Else it's always reserved,' she said.

Viveek! Who is Viveek?' asked Harshil's Mother.

Aunty, Viveek is my friend,' she replied.

But you told us that Viveek is your Gym Trainer,' said Mrs. Sahani.

Bunny raised his eyebrows.

So? Now he is my friend,'

Friend with Benefit,' whispered Bunny in Harshil's ears.

Owing to this awkward situation, Harshil's Mother stared at Mrs. Sahani with a peculiar suspicious smile.

Mr. Sahani then broke the hinge and said, She is Mrs. Rama, Harshil's Mother.'

Manshita went near her, and instead of touching her feet, she preferred to have a casual handshake.

Harshil looked at his Mother and laughed for a second because she had expected Manshita to adopt traditional Indian culture while greeting.

But instead of shaking hands, Mrs. Rama hugged Manshita.

Such gesture by her brought out a huge smile on Manshita's face and Harshil just kept glancing at her.

He felt good when she smiled.

Manshita said, Aunty, you know, I'm awfully modern girl. But such gesture from you testified that you stand way modern than me,'

There is nothing wrong if we are modern. But I don't know how to ride bike,' she said.

At this, Manshita laughed and responded, Don't worry, aunty, I'll direct you.'

Harshil felt completely ignored.

Seeing this, Bunny interrupted and said, You all are busy introducing each other, but no one will introduce my friend. I'll only have to introduce him,'

Can't your friend introduce himself?' said Manshita as she looked Harshil for the first time.

Bunny was shocked. For the first time in his life, some girl had restrained him.

Harshil felt that Manshita had shown enough of attitude by her straightforward answers.

He had to answer her, but what? — That was the question! He drew a deep breath and looked at her. I'm Harshil!' he said.

Oh Please! Say something fresh. I've read your whole bio,' she said.

How could any girl possess so much of attitude?

Harshil was cut off by her another straightforward reply. When one best friend is insulted, another one feels insulted too. Bunny felt strange, however, he had an enzyme for Harshil.

You see, they both have not communicated with each other. We can do one thing, let them talk here and we all shall remain inside and the further process,' he suggested.

But in arranged marriages, a girl and a boy can only talk after their parents exchange their mutual concerns,' remarked Mr. Sahani.

Let it be, Mr. Sahani. They both are way smarter than us.' said Mrs. Rama.

All of them moved inside and only Harshil and Manshita were left standing in the lawn outside the house.

Do you want to ask me something?' she asked as both of them began a causal walk around the lawn.

Harshil was yet mixed up in searching the topic to talk. Finally he had something to say, Can you tell me what my Mother wrote in my bio data?'

She laughed and said, Don't you know?'

No,' he replied. Was it something unusual?' he figured.

She again broke up and said, For the first time in my life I saw a bio data in which the horoscope was matched before the agreement of marriage,' What else was written?'

Your whole characteristics,'

As in?'

That includes your height, weight, skin colour, teeth colour, income, job status, Facebook status, your Instagram and Twitter follow count, your good habits, bad habits, and what not! Everything,' she responded with a friendly expression on her face.

I never knew this. I'm really sorry,' he said.

Did you see my bio data?' she asked.

No,'

Please don't lie,'

Seriously saying, your name was also a secret.'

Why so?' she asked.

Because my Mom told you're someone beyond perfect,' he said.

Didn't you even see my photo?' she queried with a lack of faith.

I didn't,'

Unbelievable man!' she exclaimed.

Looks are so important for you, aren't they?' he asked.

They are!' she responded. And let's get one point clear—I'm not a virgin,'

I'm a virgin,' said Harshil with a coy grin on his face.

She got little friendlier and inquired, Why? You found no one for fun?'

I'm not that sort of individual,' he replied.

Why? Not interested in sex?' she asked.

I mean yes, every guy is interested in that stuff,'

Awww…Then why are you a virgin?' she asked again.

I thought staying virgin would help me to grow. Sounds lame, isn't it?' he reacted.

It's little weird. How is your growth compared to your virginity?'

The same sense in which your virginity matters,' Does it actually matter?'

It doesn't. Only you matter, not your virginity.'

Hearing this, she stared into his sights and threw a nervous look. At the very next instant she drew out one of the most important questions, How much do you earn?'

I earn adequate money so as I can daily purchase bundles of condom packages,' Harshil replied.

What will I do with bundles of condom packets?' she

asked.

I don't know.' he replied. You can blow them up like balloons and play,'

Manshita vigorously laughed and said, Man, this is what I desire! I don't like somebody who is introvert and behaves as a *sharif munda*.'

But yaar, I'm a *sharif munda*. I'm a virgin,'

Okay, but do you watch porn?' she asked.

Sharif munde only watch porn,'

Learning that, she moved nearer to him and spoke, I like you, but if we line up to live together can you promise to love me?'

I don't know what love is!' he said. But today when I saw you smiling for the first time; I felt great. So maybe that's the love.' Harshil added.

She was speechless. She held onto his grasp and led inside the house. When they came in, both the families were peacefully resting in the hall and talking about something.

All of them felt strange as they saw Manshita and Harshil, hand in hand.

On seeing this, her Father, Mr. Sahani stood up and just said, Manshita......'

Harshil bhai...?' Bunny asked.

Before you all put on your individual reactions, we both need to tell you something,' she said addressing both the families.

She had something to say. But then, why did she involve Harshil into it?

We both like each other,' she said boldly.

In first ever meeting only?' inquired Mrs. Rama. What to do aunty? Your boy is someone of my type,'

This produced a running thrill of sensation in Harshil's heart. For a moment, he was convinced she was the one for whom he had waited for long.

Mr. Sahani looked at Harshil and said, Manshita is a life loving girl. Do you earn enough to meet her lifelong needs?'

I accept we are not that rich, but trust me, I have the caliber to be something remarkable one day,'

This is not a joke, kid. Life doesn't work with words! At the tail end, money talks,'

You're right uncle, money talks. It's the same money which can get us the costliest bed, but not the rest. Isn't it the very money which can buy us expensive medicines, but not health? Sex but no love! Respect in deeds, but not in spirit.'

For a moment, Mr. Sahani was quiet. Then he answered, Whatever you may assume, but still money is the true power. I'm sorry, but unless you don't earn well, we can't allow Manshita to espouse you,'

But Dad, I like him,' said Manshita interrupting her Father.

Mr. Sahani went near Harshil, and said, You're actually a nice chap. I can't neglect Manshita's choice. As a parent, I fancy her future to be free from any financial hindrances. I understand you work hard, and so can you take up one challenge from my side?'

What sort of challenge?'

I can give you nine months to prove that you're a millionaire,'

Mr. Sahani, what is this?' broke in Mrs. Rama. Mom, it's all good!' Harshil said pressing her palm. This is not fair, Mr. Sahani. Since his father passed away, all he has done is sacrifice. I can't allow him to do more sacrifices. And we're not poor. He makes enough so that your daughter can live like a queen in this house. He will always keep her smiling, yet you want him to be a millionaire? I assure you one thing—nine months are too less, but if it's a challenge, then he will undoubtedly become a millionaire one day!'

How?' Mr. Sahani asked.

When any girl leaves her native, she leaves all the sobs to her parents and brings an autumn of smile in her husband's life. Arrival of a woman changes the fate of a man in his life. She adds luck to his fortune. Same way, Manshita will add luck to Harshil's life, and they both, collectively will become millionaire one day,'

Ramaji, I adhere to what you say. I owe my gratitude to you, but still I've given him nine months to prove that he is worthy of Manshita and possibly everything.' added Mr. Sahani and took the leave from them.

That was a sort of heated discussion between the two families, but Manshita looked relaxed. When Harshil saw that relaxed face, he got a hope to at least believe he could be a millionaire!

This was their first meeting. It seemed nothing positive to either of the families, but it certainly gave Harshil a purpose to strive to become a millionaire, and tell Manshita that it was all — just for your smile.

FOR THE GIRL,
OF THE GIRL,
AND BY THE GIRL

After their family left, Bunny lost his temperament and said, How can they talk to us like that?'

Hey aunty, why are you crying?' he asked.

That was very embarrassing,' she retorted.

I told you Mom but you….' Harshil said.

Yes Harshil, you were correct!' she exclaimed.

No mom! I was wrong. You won, but how?' Harshil claimed emotionally.

How did I win, beta? I'm sorry. You had to take that insult because of me,' she regretted.

Mom, the insult was nothing in front of those few moments spent with Manshita in the lawn,'

What do you mean?'

I'm a rather ordinary guy for Manshita. She had so many reasons to turn me down on the spot. But still she liked me, and I felt special at that moment,'

How will you become a millionaire in span of just nine months?' Bunny asked.

I don't know, but now I'm well charged. *When we get a purpose in our lives, we are inspired to work more,*'

About which purpose you're talking? The very purpose which pierced you before five years,' she remarked.

It hurts when you're reminded of your grave past. It burns more, when you realize that in anger and attitude, you gave up something that could have been easily achieved. Before five years, there was that one purpose which had left Harshil with grave regret.

Partially, he had moved on from that thing. He never really wanted to think about it again and again. But when someone mentioned about the same, all the memories linked with that purpose would close in and illuminate again in his mind. This eventually made him weak.

Why is our past haunting? Shouldn't it go permanently away from our memory? But it doesn't go. Why? Past and present are completely different period. Still why does the past influence our present?

The reason is simple: our past is the manifestation to our future. What happens when a stone is thrown in a stagnant water logged source? Initially, it creates ripples on the water surface, and after sometime the water becomes stationary as it was before. Such is our life.

Assume that the action of projecting stone in the water is your past. Due to the effect of the action, the ripples were formed on the water surface — this is the present.
In past, an action of throwing stone resulted into the reaction of ripple production in the present. So in this way, the past influenced the present.

Now think, does this whole process have any result or influence on the future? Absolutely not!
No matter how many stones are thrown till the butt end of the power, at last a person would stop, and thus no ripples would be created. That indeed will be our future.

Same situation was also applicable to Harshil. One mistake in the past was depriving him to become a millionaire in his present.

Before meeting Manshita and her family, Harshil had no solid purpose in his life. But that day when Manshita came, he realized that his purpose and happiness were hidden deep inside her smile.

He never grasped why, but every part of his body was willingly ready to do everything for Manshita. Instead, he was motivated to do something—just for her smile.

At the other hand, his Mother and his friend Bunny thought that Harshil was trapped in the maze of attraction. Becoming a millionaire in short space was surely an impossible thing.

Don't you trust me guys?' Harshil said, as he looked in their eyes.

Instead of arguing, both of them just embraced him with love. Don't you live for this day? Well, you obviously do. Your dreams get ignited when the ones near you are the first set of people to support you.

Anyone can verbally assure you for the support, but only a few people can physically prove it. If you ever had such person in your life, then adore them because they are the ones ready to bring about anything—just for your smile!

☺

The days were swiftly passing as Harshil began the stint to track down that one ultimate opportunity for an interview in some multinational company.

Initially, he went through the news cuttings, and called the numbers one by one. But the salary proposed was much less than his current income. Still, he decided not to give up and daily continue the same thing.

One day he received a call from an unknown number.

Hello…!' he said.

Meet me in five minutes!'

What? Who's this?'

Don't ask anything. Meet me at Hauz Khas Café. Bye.'

When the call got over, he realized that it was none other than Manshita.

Why had I not taken her number?' he questioned himself.

Nevertheless, Manshita wanted to meet him, and he was excited.

Life takes a massive turn with an entry of a girl. Every flower is beautiful, but still it is differentiated by the quality of essence present in it. Same way, the arrival of a girl in one's life yields an essence of love and passion.

☺

Hauz Khas Café

This was the first time Harshil would meet a girl alone and since it was his first date, he preferred to be on time.

Harshil…' she spoke from behind.

He swung around to get her, and the beautiful voice was enough to assure her presence.

Manshita was beautiful, but that day she looked totally hot.

Silver coloured one-piece, which was shimmering due to shy white light of moon, plus the spell of her black eyeliner interpreted her hotness. Harshil shifted his eyes down—just to have a sharp peek at her sexy milky legs.

Even before he could praise her, she said, Let me tell you one thing. Since I'm a very beautiful girl, I'm very melodramatic too,'

Oh! No problem, accepted,' he added giving her a warm smile.

You engineers are quite serious. Can't you guys give a casual hug instead of this cute little smile?'

Accumulating the courage to have a peep at her sexy legs was a hard thing for Harshil, and now, she was asking him for a hug.

Leaving out all the restraints, he got hold of her hands and they had a short three second embrace. She sensed something and asked, Don't tell me that this was the first time you hugged a girl?'

Exactly!'

However, in order to break the immature jinx, Harshil asked her, Why suddenly the desire to meet me?'

Actually my all friends are busy, and so I was getting bored. You were the only contact left in my cell which I knew would never disappoint me. So I called you to hang out with me,'

That's right! I hardly disappoint anyone,'

Now stop buttering me,' she said as they both sat on those long chairs in the café.

I'm terrible when it comes to start any talk; you only say.' Harshil said.

She pouted her cheeks and said, I'm highly sensitive girl. I get hurt so easily,'

Don't worry; I'll never hurt you,'

Six guys before you also said the same,'

What?' he asked. I mean six guys?'

Haanji… Six guys and guess what? I rejected each and every one of them,' she replied giving a hi-fi.

Harshil felt little curious. So he asked her, On what

ground you rejected them?'

You know, I just hate cheesy guys. And unfortunately all of them were cheesy. They had low sense of humor and were extremely dramatic,'

In what sense they were dramatic?'

As you know, I'm eighteen plus non-virginal girl, and still they addressed me as babe. Come on, that's fucking annoying,' she said.

To score further relish to the fury, a waiter interrupted her and asked, Beautiful lady, can I bring you something?'

Yah, do me a favor. One packet of condom, please,' she responded.

Excuse me?' asked the waiter with a fiendish look.

And then I'll draw that condom right up on your pervert eyes, and I'll see if you still have the balls to stalk any girl like that,'

It was an ultimate insult a guy could never vision in his dreams.

Oh come on dude, don't take it seriously,' she said as she stood up and gave him a short sensible hug and asked for forgiveness.

That feels good!' waiter exclaimed.

And now, if you're over it, can you bring a glass of water, and just fuck off from here?' she said staring at that waiter.

The waiter felt super insulted and quietly passed away. For sure, he was not to be seen again for a brief time.

Harshil went to the counter and ordered hot chocolate for both of them.

You can be full of melodrama, and a guy can't be? That's cruel,' Harshil said.

Fuck yes. If a guy works in melodramatic way, then it

shows the size of his dick,' she said.

You know this better since you're not a virgin!' Harshil commented with a smile on his face.

I hope that it wasn't a taunt. Let me tell you, I hate the guys who keep lamenting me,' she said.

No, it wasn't a taunt. But seriously tell me that how did you lose your virginity? Because I was not a night-out guy during my adolescence,'

The facial expressions on her face changed as she told him, You guys speculate that a girl who has lost her virginity to some guy has no feelings, but you should also be cognizant of the fact that she only surrenders her body to the one she really adores. I don't know about other girls, but I had only lost my virginity once and that with a guy, whom I loved,'

And who was he?'

My boyfriend number three, Riyan.'

Boyfriend number three?' Harshil asked. What about boyfriend number one and two?'

Manshita laughed and said, Those guys were not so special. I mean, there was nothing like relationship with them. It was just a mere time pass.' she said. But Riyan....He was something special,' she added.

How did you both meet?' Harshil asked.

It all began in the first year of the college. When you're new to the college, the first basic thing you figure out is the handsome hunk. He was the one that I felt was the most attractive guy ever seen at the first sight in the college that day.' she let it out as her eyes were lost in his image.

You know about the orientation ceremony of the college, right?'

Yah,'

So luckily that day he had seated in the first row, and I was right behind him. Let me tell you, an erotic perfume aroma is also enough to seduce a girl like me, and he smelt sexy that day. Later on, when the groups we were formed according to the roll numbers, I was so happy to have in my group and that was when all just set up,'

Let me guess, as expected it started with a friend request?' Harshil guessed.

Fuck no!'

Then may be on some dating site?'

I keep myself away from the stigma of social media. It all started at the Fresher's party,' she said.

So what happened at the Fresher's party?'

I will tell you everything, but not here. Let's go for a walk.'

As they were leaving the café, the same waiter with whom Manshita had acted rudely turned to Harshil and said, Sir, your hot chocolate is ready,'

Manshita showed him the middle finger, and flung off, You only drink that, honey!'

☺ ☺ ☺

YOU'RE SWEET; I'LL NEVER CHEAT

As they began the walk, Harshil asked, So you were saying something about the Fresher's party?'

That was the most memorable day of my life,' she said. To me, Riyan seemed rather shy, but his hotness was the main gossip for all the girls over there that night.'

What made him so marked amongst the girls?'

Black magic, Bitch. It was a black magic! Six foot tall, fair in complexion, muscular symmetry, sharp jaw line, and that black tuxedo was more than enough to hold my mind for rest of the night,'

Yes, but what followed at that night?' Harshil asked.

You might be acquainted with the tradition of the Fresher's party,' she told.

The seniors bully you to do some act as a part of dare. Mostly, in our Mechanical, as only boys are there, sometimes the acts become very shameful,' he replied.

Something similar also happened to
me.' Like what?'

A pole dance!' she exclaimed.

Harshil got little jealous this time and asked, Who was the pole? And who danced?'

Of course Riyan was the pole and any one girl was to be chosen randomly for the dance. Fortunately, I was taken up by the seniors,'

Oh! Fortunately? And you must have agreed to with no hesitation?'

Right. Also, the seniors told me that if I had done that task, the tag of Miss Fresher would be mine and Riyan would be Mr. Fresher,'

Just go on. Don't stop. Let me hear the worst.' Harshil said.

He was forced to stand upright like a pole. An insignificant alteration would have earned him birthday bums in advance. So as he was standing still, I came forward, and stood ahead of him. He looked into my eyes, and I looked in his eyes. Everything appeared to be so perfect, but still none of us uttered a single word. The seniors then ordered me to do a few steps of pole dance on him. As I came closer to him, I felt super nervous. My heart began to beat up, but once again that trace of the perfume was an enigma to keep me going. I rested my arms around his neck, and came much closer to him. Seeing that, he preferred to close his eyes because he knew what he was experiencing was not less than heaven. To generate the first step of the pole dance, I stuck my whole body over his muscular physic. For the second step, I put my right leg over his belly. While I was doing so, my joints accidentally touched his manhood, and I felt something terribly hard. He was excited, and to be honest, the same thing was going on inside my body. Then for the final step of the pole dance, I swung my hair over his skull so that it covered his face. For a few seconds, there was an absolute darkness around us. And we both saw each other, eye to eye, for the first time. He smiled for the very first time beneath the darkness of my hair. As I was standing on my heels, I lost my balance. And while I was falling, I intentionally parted my lips over his lips to create a gentle touch. Yes, it was a sign that I was falling for him.'

Harshil patiently heard the whole Fresher's party scene, but he didn't know what to react! He was surprised, but at the same time he felt little detached from inside.

Looking at his changed facial grimaces, Manshita said, I know, it feels rather awkward and strange but this was what I am. You also have the full liberty to leave. I'm no one to waste your time.'

Do you know why my facial expressions suddenly changed?'

You didn't like my pole dance incident with Riyan. That's why,'

No Manshita. It's not like that. I felt so bad for myself,' he said.

What?'

Can you expect anything like that from the Fresher's party of Mechanical Engineering?'

She laughed as she understood his point and said, Absolutely nothing more than the desperate dicks. But I always used to like the guys from the Mechanical Engineering. They make sincere attempts to talk with a girl they llike,'

You see something positive in every negative situation. That's the point I love about you.'

She winkled her lips, but said nothing.

You didn't tell me how you lost your virginity?' Harshil asked.

Why are you so keen about that stuff?'

Are you going to tell me or not?'

Okay, then listen...So after that pole dance got over, we both felt so embarrassed that we didn't say a single word till the end of the party. Later on, as expected, we both were crowned Mr. & Miss Fresher respectively. Riyan approached me, and asked for a click. With no hesitation, I agreed.

It was so enthralling when his hand moved around my back during the whole course of the photo shoot. After taking the dinner, he asked me for a casual walk in the park nearby. We discussed about each other's passion, likes, dislikes, and then suddenly this happened —

Riyan said, —Your hair. They are so silky and beautiful. I'm falling for it,‖

—I'm too falling for your black tuxedo,‖ I replied at that instant.

—You're hot. Seriously, you're!‖ Riyan said as he gave the clear signals.

—Don't flirt. Just tell me what you want?‖ I asked him.

To which he replied, —I cannot tell you what I want. I can just do it,‖

I said, —Okay, let me know what you can do.‖

He took me in his arms, and I knew what would happen then. I closed my eyes because I wanted it to happen. He was rather soft and slow in his action, and I could sense that softness when his lips had an impact on my lower lip. My resilience got over, as my limbs went over his head, and blew his lips passionately. He went one step ahead as he kissed me on the neck. Gradually, his fingers reached inside my body. And soon after that ultimate pleasure happened till I was perfectly wet,'

Manshita further extended, After that incident, he often demanded to have fun. I asked for a relationship and commitment, and he agreed to it with no reluctance,' How was the relationship?' Harshil asked.

In the beginning, every relationship appears to be perfect, but as the time passes—needs and responsibilities depict the entire scenario of your love.' she said.

He was sweet in the beginning. I can say — beyond awesome. With each passing day, he ensured my trust, and so finally one day he had the virginity as well. So many photos together, hang outs, coffee shops, silent dates, long drives, long kisses, phone sex, laughing, crying and then again smiling — our relationship was splendid,'

Then what led to the break up?' Harshil asked curiously.

One email from an unknown person changed everything,' she said.

What was there in that mail?'

Her eyes grew moist as she replied, There was one girl, who sent me her pictures with Riyan,'

So what was bad in that?'

Both of them were in a stage of intimacy.' she answered. Later, I received a video featuring few more girls around him. All of them were having fun.'

Harshil was stunned. He thought how could anyone cheat like that? We don't love a person to see such a day in our life. Manshita had seen it. She was down on her knees sobbing.

Harshil went down and assured her, Are you okay?' Riyan still follows me. He tries to call me. Frequently sends a text message, but I don't reply. I just don't want his presence in my life.' she let out.

Don't cry, Manshita.'

Why? Let me cry.'

I never imagined even you can cry,'

Shut up.' she said. Even I'm little sentimental. I'm strong, but that doesn't mean that my tears don't flow,'

Now close your eyes. I've got something that will set

up your mood!' he said.

What do you have?'

Not like this,' Harshil said as he wrapped up his fist over her radiant eyes.

He drew the dark chocolate from of his pocket and placed it on her lap.

Can you guess?' he asked.

Kohinoor!' she exclaimed.

Fuck!'

ManForce?'

Come on,'

It must be Score then,'

Are you mad?'

Okay, now the final guess. It's Kamasutra,'

Harshil got upset and uncovered her eyes. Manshita was blank when she looked at that dark chocolate.

Are you a condom franchise?' Harshil asked her.

No, Harshil. The truth is — till date I've only got such varieties of surprises,' she answered and as she said so, a drop of tear glided down from her eyes and fell flat on Harshil's thumb.

Harshil offered her the chocolate and said, Dark chocolate improves the mood. Have it, you will definitely feel good,'

For the first time, she gave him a heartfelt smile and remarked, All the guys I've dated have either bored me or made me go crazy. You're the only one who made me smile.'

She opened the wrapper and put one piece of chocolate in his mouth. These chocolates are the proof that every guy till date has only used me,'

I'm not like those guys,'

All fucking guys are the same! When they get what they want, they turn their back. Tell me then what's bad if I kiss someone? What's wrong if I make out with someone else? Will you still trust me?' she asked him a grave question.

Yes, I will.'

How is that reasonable? You've never been in a relationship before. You know nothing about trust,'

I agree I don't know, but when you shared this chocolate with me, I felt secured. May be that's the sole sense of trust I understand. Trust is sharing. Isn't that sufficient for you?' Harshil said.

It's more than enough,' she said and curled her fingers in his wreath.

But never cheat upon me,' he said.

Some guys are creep; that's why we

cheat,' What do you think about me?'

You're sweet, I'll never cheat.' she responded.

After having a deep and touchy conversation, both of them continued their walk without saying a word.

From this whole unexpected journey with Manshita, he realized that girls get emotionally broken up when the person whom they love, is the same person who cheats upon them. But once, when a girl like Manshita moves ahead, then she is also the strongest.

A girl needs your attention, but once when they ignore; you strive for their attention. Sex is not their want; instead a person of correct sex' is their want.

In our society, there are many girls like Manshita who have dealt with the similar cause, or possibly even wickeder than that. But still carrying all that, they reveal a smile on their face advocating that everything is fine in their lives!

That's why SHE' is the God's noblest boon, regardless of any form. What can she ask from you if she is the only one who has created you? She has everything but still she only desires one thing. Efforts!

Efforts which can set forth that they were only intended — just for your smile!

☺ ☺ ☺

NO CHATTING, ONLY DATING

Each succeeding day brought Harshil and Manshita much closer. Technology decreases the gap of formal communication in modern era, but Manshita was a person who didn't believe in chatting.

According to her, chatting was a myth that could only trap a person under false impression of words. She believed that the real nature of a person could only be determined, face to face. So whenever they felt like talking to each other, they used to either meet up, or have a video call on Skype.

☺

Since Manshita had to go out of the town for few days, she wanted to meet Harshil before departing. They decided to meet in the evening at the Deer Park which is located in Hauz Khas of south Delhi which is one of the most fascinating spots for the duos in Delhi.

This time Manshita reached on time, but Harshil didn't. This delay was spoiling her mood because she had been waiting for more than half an hour.

I'm very sorry. The traffic at this hour is horrible,' said Harshil.

You could have text me about the same,' she said.

No chatting, only dating. You only said this,'

She smiled and said, You're very smart. Those are my words, and you're using them to butter me?'

Harshil held her hand, and both of them sat down on the green grass.

So where are you going?' he asked.
I've to go to Kolkata for one important
work,' When are you coming back?'
Awh come on! Are we here to discuss
that?' Ummmm…then discuss what?'
Anything,' she said gripping her lips.
Can I ask you something? This question is droning in
my head since long,'

She agreed, as she offered him cream and onion
chips. Do you still love Riyan?'

The biting reflex on her lips suddenly stopped when
she heard that remark. Still she composed herself and
replied, You know, some questions do really hurt,'

It's all right. You need not say a single word that
troubles you. I'm sorry,'

Harshil, at present my life is beautiful. He is out of
my life. If I say anything about him, it doesn't imply that I
love him. He is a dark cloud I'll never forget, nor forgive. I
expected the water in form of rain, and he gave it in form
of tears,'

I understand Manshita. I'm deeply
sorry!' I need to tell you something!' she
said. Sure,'
Whatever I'm about to say is related to
you,' And what is that?'
I don't love him anymore, but I love someone
else,' What? Seriously?' Harshil asked with joy.
She bit her jaws and said, Yes,'

Although Harshil expressed the joy on his face, but
deep inside the heart he was quite broken. He had begun
to love her, and instantly everything was against him.

So who is that lucky guy?' he asked looking at the

other way, as his eyes were suffused with water.

I told his name in the beginning,' she

remarked. No, you didn't.'

I said that whatever I'm about to say is something related to you,'

A jolt of emotion coursed down his body when he realized to what she pointed. The lacerated heart sprang to rejoin again.

Does that mean that you love me?'

She felt shy. In order to respond him about the same, she rolled down her eyes. After few instants when she opened it, the dark liner got spitted into two bands, suggesting that she loved him.

How can you love me?' Harshil asked as the sustained water from the eyes rained down.

I have no reasons for that.' she said.

I'm not too rich to fulfill all the desires you want,' he said.

I want you, not the desires. At this point, I realize that some dreams never see their fate alone. If you're with me, we will work for each other's dream. We will add each other,' she suggested.

That's fine, but I'm not too handsome as well,' You're

handsome, but more than that you're cute' she
said stretching his cheeks.

I don't think so,'

It doesn't matter what you think,' she said mocking Dwayne Johnson — The Rock, of WWE.

Are you truly ready to love someone again?' Harshil asked holding her hand.

Yes. Even I'm bit confused. Why do we love someone again despite of learning we were hurt then?' she asked.

Well, it's simple. We all will die one day; nevertheless we still live and breathe. If we can't stop living, then why should we stop loving?' he replied.

Second chance in love was a solid redemption for me. But now, after meeting you; it's just a sweet respect,' she said.

Harshil looked in her eyes and said, Love is a very strong word. I want you to take all the time you want before making this decision. It's true I always wanted to have a person like you in my life. I can wait for some time more, because I may not be your destiny, but for me; you are my damn destination.

He said, It's true; our way of living is different. I'm not like you, but I wish to end my life with someone like you. It's said: Don't wait for a perfect moment. Take a moment, and make it perfect. I want to become that perfect moment for you.'

Harshil....' she said placing her hands over his shoulders.

I don't know what to say. I just love you, and that's the only thing I can do,' he stated.

Say nothing more,' she said and opened her arms Idiot. Just hug me.'

☺

Mostly, the first hug is a soft one, but it was not so in their case. When do we hug someone tight?

We hug someone tight only when we feel apart. In spite of being surrounded by so many people, in some way or the other way, both of them were alone.

Do you know the reason why you are so special to me?' she asked as still she was there in the warmth of his arms.

I don't know. I wonder how you even like me since I'm not someone of your type,' he said.

You have no idea about the worst feeling in this world! It is the feeling that holds us to trust someone again. It stops us from falling in love once again. You're the one who shattered that feeling from me. That's why you're so special.'

She added, We realize the value of our tears, the day we get someone who never lets it shed. I guess that I've got that someone in you.'

Her words were building her respect in his eyes.
A girl is lucky if she has a guy who can make her feel special. But luckier is a guy whose girl can make him feel special.

What happens when the water is poured on the soil? Initially, the water stays on, but gradually soil absorbs all the water beneath it. Same thing is also relevant for love.

When the water of trust and acceptance touches the heart, two people absorb their feelings into each other, and the plant called Love' is born.

☺

That day Manshita made him realize that if you love someone; you don't need to be in a secured relationship. All you need is trust and acceptance to stay there for each other. Love sees no relationship. Love only sees a person, and Manshita was becoming that person for Harshil.

At that instance, Harshil murmured, Whatsoever happens; I'll be always there for you,'

Did you say something?' she asked.

Yes,'

But what?'

Nothing,' he said

Pagal!' she exclaimed pulling his cheeks.

Have you observed something around us?' Harshil asked her.

She looked perplexed.

Harshil pointed his index finger towards one little boy and said, Every time when we meet; I see this small kid around us,'

Manshita had a look over that kid. She spun around and said, But I never saw him,'

Trust me. I frequently see him, and I'm damn sure about it. He always has this sketchbook and a pencil in his fist,'

Sketching must be his hobby. So he must be here to draw something related to park. Leave him alone,' she said.

At last when Manshita had to leave, she asked, Do you trust me, Harshil?'

He held her fingers and said, Of course, I do!'

I intend to claim you believe in me as a whole, right?' Yes, but what happened?'

She sank her eyes.

Perceiving this, Harshil asked, What happened, Manshita?'

Ummm… I want your help.'

Harshil nodded, and replied, You need not ask for; you just have to say,'

I'm in need of 10,000 rupees for some procedures, but at present, I don't have cash. Tomorrow I've to go for Kolkata, so can you help me?' she asked.

Harshil was blank for a time. He felt, for what sort of procedures she needed 10,000 rupees? Looking at his aged body language, Manshita said, Hey, it's all fair. You don't worry; I'll handle it.'

She turned around and begun to walk. Harshil held her limp hand and said, Did I say no?'

He reached for his wallet and put it her hands, and said, I've only this much cash,'

You trust is so rich that you gave me your whole wallet?'

When I said I trust you; ensure that it's forever,'

Before he could say anything further, she positioned her lips over his lips, and gave a gentle kiss.

Harshil had experienced all things in his life with open eyes, but the impression of that kiss had forced him to shut down his eyes.

☺

Why do we close our eyes while kissing someone?

Well, perhaps the answer for this is also the question that why do we close our eyes while praying to God?

Eyes are closed during the prayer because it's a peace seeking plea to the Almighty. On the other hand, we endure the very desired peace during the kiss; so that's the reason our eyes get shut during the kiss.

☺

She took out the money from his wallet.

I'm sorry. I don't have 10,000 rupees. Whatever money is there you can take it,' he stated.

There were five thousand rupees in his wallet. She took four thousand rupees and put it in her fancy purse.

But how will you manage the remaining money?' he asked.

Don't worry. I'll see. This will help me a lot,' she told.

She then took out one yellow spongy smiley ball from her purse and placed it in his hands.

What's this?' he asked.

47

This is very special thing. When we help someone, we engender a smile on their face. You've helped me and made me smile, so I've shared my smile with you. This yellow sponge ball is the symbol of that smile,'

Then I would love to help you every time,' he added.

Think and say. Helping me is not that simple. You'll be bankrupt,'

You also think and say!'

Why?'

Because you don't know, I can do anything...' Anything?'

Just for your smile.' he declared and kissed her temple.

LET US TAKE IT THAT WAY

Manshita went to Kolkata, and that was the point when everything set up. The place at which Harshil had been working was nowhere near to the stipulation of a millionaire' target set by Mr. Sahani for marrying Manshita. To cope up that depression, Harshil wanted to drink. Bunny secretly arranged whisky bottles at his home, and they both made a plan to booze-up that evening.

Looking at his face, Bunny asked, Why are you looking so upset?'

You're pretending as if you know nothing. Days are slipping away, and still I'm unable to discover that ideal job to throw the money on the face of her father,'

Do the hand job. That's the best remedy in any problem,'

Will you fuck off?'

Relax, boy. You still have nine months to prove. Till then, let's just dream,' said Bunny.

Dream about what?'

To dream for that absolute life; full of gold, and no stress. You know, even I aspire to become the richest man in this world one day,'

Harshil clapped and said, You're already an asshole. So come back to the reality,'

Don't get depressed. I see, this millionaire task is next to impossible for non IITians like us, but we need to keep trying.' Bunny said.

As soon as Harshil heard the word IIT, old wave of dejection passed over his heart. Bunny knew the reason of that grief. He rested his paw over Harshil's collar, and said, I'm sorry. I shouldn't have talked about IIT,'

Two marks of difference, and I was denied from studying there,' Harshil reacted the tears fell down in the glass of whisky.

There was a brief silence. Harshil broke the silence by saying, This difference of two marks is still stopping me to go ahead in my life,'

We can't fight with our own faith. I wish we were not born in the General category,' Bunny said.

On hearing this, Harshil closed his eyes, and the old pictures flashed back in his head.

IIT result 2006-2007

Name: Harshil Joshi

Physics: 25/120

Chemistry: 70/120

Mathematics: 50/120

Grand total: 145/360

Cut off criteria –

General: 147/360

OBC: 120/360

SC: 100/360

ST: 70/360

(*YOU ARE NOT ELIGIBLE TO QUALIFY.)

This was the result that had deprived Harshil from studying at IIT. At that time, his mother sympathized him stating that he had sought his best, and she was very proud of him. But he knew, she was unhappy. Her wish to see him in IIT was left short just because of these two marks. However, he had the chance to study at some NIT institute. But he didn't prefer it because when you dream for the sky; you simply aspire to fetch your own place in the sky, and not in the stars that are located at the fixed place.

So in the anger, he took the decision of not studying at the NIT, and undoubtedly he had to pay the price for it. He was left with no other option expect to study at some local engineering college, and perhaps this step was the end of his dream.

Bunny suddenly rose up.

What happened?' Harshil asked.

Do you know one old school

rule?' Which rule?' Harshil asked

When you don't get your rights, just snatch

it,' What do you mean?'

You'll go to the IIT placement cell, and give an interview for the job,' Bunny said.

Are you nuts? How will I get in?'

It's a three-step process. First of all, you have to enter the college, secondly you need to figure out about the companies coming for the placement, and last, you have to enter the placement cell for giving an interview for recruitment,'

It is so easy, isn't it? Harshil mocked.

It might sound insane, but once you're in the placement cell, nothing will stop you unless you complete your interview.'

But how will I get in?'

Tell me, what's the primary thing you require to enter any institute?' Bunny asked

Identity card!' Harshil exclaimed.

Excellent! So all we have to do is make your fake ID card,'

That's so risky. How will you manage?'

You require to make small investment. I know some agents who create illegal documents in the return of money,'

How much do they charge?' Harshil asked.

I don't know. May be anything around five to ten thousands,'

Yaar Bunny… There is little

problem,' What happened?'

At present, I don't have enough money to do all this,' Harshil said. Actually Manshita needed some money. It was an emergency. So whatever personal expense I had, I gave it to her,' he added.

Fuck! This girl is driving you crazy.' Bunny said

I know,' responded Harshil with a smile on his face.

Look dude, you can't give your money to anyone like that.'

She is not anyone, and she was in need of it,'

Did you inquire for what purpose she wanted the money?' Bunny asked

No,'

Did she promise to return the

money?' I don't know!'

Damn! I can't believe that an understanding person like you can also be confined,' Bunny said.

She has not trapped me. She really needed
it,' How can you be so sure?'

Lips can lie, eyes can never lie.' Harshil said.

You've gone crazy. Nevertheless, it was my duty to
warn you.'

Harshil placed his palm over Bunny's shoulder and
said, 'I really admire your concern, but she is not like other
girls,'

That's the problem. You've never experienced other
girls in your life as she is the first one,'

She will never hurt me!'

I wish that she never troubles you, but....'

Bunny, we both love each other,'

I wonder what you guys are up to!'

*We're absolutely doing nothing. There are no promises, no
commitments, no reasons, and no confusions between us. I lead
her, and she builds me – that's our relationship.'*

How can you love her so much?' Bunny asked.

Money cannot sustain any relation. Some relations
don't give us any profit, yet they make us rich. Her
presence is such richness in my life.'

Bunny had nothing more to say. He worried a lot
about Harshil and that's the reason he was against
Manshita.

*We are lucky if we have friends who suspect on the person we
love because they wonder how did we manage to find someone
who could love us more in their comparison?*

After the emotional blend of feelings, both of them
were back to the business. Bunny tried to contact a few
agents who had been making illegal ID cards. But when
they told the agents to prepare a false ID card for IIT, they
used to cut the call.

Not a single one of them were ready to do such a risky task.

But eventually, after trying for six long hours, they got an appointment from one agent who agreed to meet them at the Hazrat Nizamuddin Railway Station, the following day.

☺

Hazrat Nizamuddin Station

Harshil and Bunny reached at the decided place just before fifteen minutes of the actual time.

H. Nizamuddin Station is one of the liveliest places in Delhi. They thought how was it possible to have the convention for an unauthorized operation in such a chic area? But in an overpopulated country as India, things work like that only.

If you have to rise at the top level, you have to fall at the bottom. But if you want to rise at the top level illegally, you have to fall at the third grade level legally.' Harshil thought in his mind.

He knew the work which he was about to do would be a cheating upon himself, but it was the *love* that had propelled him to do so and he was ready for the cause.
His luck had cheated him by just two marks, and now, he was ready to challenge his future by the means of this illegal act.

Minutes later, a guy dressed as a salesman approached them, and asked in soft tone, IIT?'

Harshil was confused. He looked at Bunny who thought it must be a code word to communicate. Both of them shook their heads in affirmation.

The guy was little relieved as he said, My name is Parth. I guess you are the boys who asked for that fake ID card?'

Yes, we did.' Bunny said.

Let us discuss the things peacefully at that tea stall,' he said.

He took them at one tea stall on the station, and said in typical Delhitie manner, Babbu... Teen strong cutting bannaiyo...'

However Babbu, the tea maker responded from the behind, Agaya Ch***** firse!'

Harshil felt little strange. Bunny smiled and said, Welcome to the real Delhi,'

Indeed,' responded Parth. Here the day never begins, if you don't abuse.' he added.

Are you the one who will do the work for us?' Harshil asked him.

He laughed and said, No, no! I'm only an agent. I work for such illegal organizations and serve the clients to them.'

So we are your clients?' Bunny asked.

You are my customers. Let us take it that way,' responded Parth.

Parth was an agent, but he had the elements which a salesman would merely possess. His way of speaking, his actions, and gestures were adequate to judge that he was something big.

Can you brief me about the task?' he asked.

Bunny took a sip of tea and said, This is my friend, Harshil. The task is simple. He wants to go to IIT. So you've to make a fake ID card for him to enter inside the campus,'

IIT? And why only IIT? Are you guys serious? Aukat hai tumhari?'

Parth would be an intermediate in this entire thing. So

Harshil felt that everything should be crystal clear. Parth was astonished when he learned that Harshil was taking such a big chance just to marry a girl.

How could any person do such a deed to marry someone?' he asked Harshil.

Harshil thought not to answer that, and instead asked him, Are you going to work for us? Yes or No.'

The thing which you're asking me to work for is next to impossible. IIT's are directly hooked up to the Education Ministry, Government of India. Even if we touch the foundation, whole building can fall upon us,'

So it's impossible?'

Yes, it's impossible,' Parth said. But I can try. I never give up. Just give me a few days as I have to search for the people who can undertake your work. Then only something can happen,' he responded.

What will we do till then?' asked Bunny staring at his friend.

Well, till then you can prepare Harshil for this risky task,'

All right!' Harshil said. How much do we have to pay you for all this?' he asked.

Are you truly doing this for one girl?' Parth asked. Yes,'

Why? I mean to say, girls come and go. You need not take such a huge risk for a girl,'

You're right, my friend. Girls come and go away from our lives, but she isn't a girl. She appends a meaning of sensible woman to a girl. That's the reason I'm ready to do all this,'

I will advise you to think again. You have no idea what can happen to you if you're caught. The punishment will be severe,' Parth warned him.

Punishment? Oh yes, I'm all set for it,'

He had gone mad!' exclaimed Bunny.

Harshil looked at Bunny and said, What doesn't kill you, keeps you going. I have no fear.'

So Parth, let's talk about the money,' Bunny

said. Not less than ten thousand rupees!'

Are you crazy? I'm just asking you for an ID card. Not for the graduation certificate of IIT,' Bunny said.

Graduation certificate would have charged less, but the thing you're demanding requires capital,'

Before Harshil could ask anything, Bunny finalized the deal by shaking hands with Parth, and gave him an initial token for the task.

Later on, Parth noted all the personal details of Harshil that were needed to be printed on the ID card, and promised them to call back as soon as possible.

☺

Where were you?' asked his Mother, as Harshil reached the home late that day.

Come on, Mom! Grow up.' he said.

Harshil, I need to discuss something.' she said, arranging his plate for the dinner.

As he sat on the chair, she said, The thing I'm about to say might hurt you, but trust me, it's the best for you, me and ultimately us,'

What happened?'

Forget Manshita!' she said.

As soon she said so, his wigs lit up.

What did you just say?' he asked.

In a cordial way, she placed her palm on his head and said, It's better for us, if you can forget Manshita. You both can't marry eachother,'

And that was it. His anger had reached its climax. In anxiety he stood up, and as a result the chair fell down.

His Mother got tensed and tried to console him by saying, You like Manshita, but you can't be together. I'm sorry, I was the one to tell you that she was the perfect girl, but now I don't see your happiness with her. I can't see you striving daily for that millionaire mark,'

Harshil forcefully banged his hand on the glass plate. Everything on the table got wracked into the pieces. Enraged, he tore the tablecloth, and threw the food containers down on the floor.
His Mother kept shouting, but he didn't listen.
Tears railed from his eyes when he said, What do you think of yourself, mom? Don't I hold any right on my life?'

He said, You decided a school for me. I went there and studied. Fine, I had to agree. You told me that science has future. Fine, I agreed. You wanted me to work hard for IIT. Fine, I even accepted that but what did I receive? Nothing more expect regretting because of those two bloody marks. Fine, I remained quiet. Then one day, you suddenly told me to marry someone because you wanted me to see happy. Fine, without even looking at the her face, I agreed. And then today, you're telling me to leave her with no proper reason.'

The thing is, you have no reason left to cherish in your life. You want me to live a life where I'll simply keep rubbing your tears but who will care for my tears, Mom? Who will wipe them off after you go?'

Before Harshil could say anything more, she blasted out her tears. She ran inside the room, picked up the photo of her husband, and hugged it. Her tears feel on the photo frame as she kept sobbing.

I hate you, Mom! You still love Dad, regardless of his existence in this world. Even though God has separated him from us, I never tried to separate you from him. Ask me, how I feel every single time when you weep under his image? Despite of all this, I never stop you because I know you still love him. Then how did you think of separating me from Manshita? You know I love her.' She said nothing but kept crying.

I feel like a wreck, just living for you and our desires. Till now, I thought you cared for my happiness. But I was mistaken. You only think about yourself, and your future,'

She moved her hand over the photo frame and replied, If your dad was here today, he would have surely slapped you for disrespecting me,'

You're right. He would have slapped me,' he said. Not for disrespecting you, but for slandering my personal dreams which I kept aside, just for your smile.' he added.

DARE NOT CALL HER A BITCH

After that conflict with his Mother, Harshil left the home. He always needed a peaceful place to settle his mind after such conflicts. And it was during this emptiness, he missed his Father.

Mother and Father are the most valuable aspect in one's life. There are like two sides of a coin. One gives undying love, and the other gives immense protection. Love cannot survive without protection, and protection can never exist without love.

Harshil was missing that protection in his life. He always needed someone who would say——Go; move ahead in your life. If you fall, I'm there to pick you up.‖

But every single time when he fell down, he had to get up on his own and move ahead because there was no protection to boost him.

Harshil!' said Bunny from behind. Come on Harshil, let's go home!'

Why did you come here? Just leave me alone,'

I went to your home, and I saw that aunty was crying. I can't believe you're disrespecting your Mother for that girl,'

Harshil said nothing.

Dude, she's a bitch! Leave her. Let me tell you something straight—she is gold digger.' Bunny said.

For a moment, Harshil couldn't believe it was his best friend who was saying all that. Bunny patted him on his shoulder and said, Leave her. She's a bitch,'

This enraged Harshil. He got hold of Bunny's collar and said, Shut up! One more word against her, and I'll bang you,'

Bunny also got excited and said, I will not allow you to wreck your life behind that bitch,' Harshil dragged him down on the floor.

Don't you dare call her a bitch! Who are you to say that? You're a loser. You can't love any girl. That's the reason your past relationships were solely based on…,'

That's what I'm saying you. Have sex, and forget her,' Tears fell down from Harshil's eyes as he said, I cannot believe you're my best friend,'

Watching him cry, Bunny stood up, and came forward to hug him. He did the same every single time when they fought. But this time, it would not happen. No sooner did he move forward, Harshil slapped him hard.

Bunny was flabbergasted. He placed his palm on his right cheek which was tightly slapped by his bestie.
You would never see a tear in Bunny's eyes, but not this time. He sat down on his knees, and just wondered to what had just transpired.

Just go away from here. I need no one in my life,' Harshil said.

Bunny stood up and expected Harshil to have a look at him but there was an absolute ignorance from the opposite end. Bunny left, and Harshil thought that it was an end of the so-called everlasting friendship.
He had heard that Friendship was greater than love, but he never thought his love would one day kill his friendship.

Harshil always carried a laptop in the side bag of his bike. He opened his laptop and made a skype call to Manshita. He desperately needed to talk with her.

As soon as the screen flashed in, Harshil asked her, When are you coming back?'
She got little worried on seeing Harshil's appearance and asked, Where are you? You're not at home and wait, your eyes are wet! What happened?'

Manshita, everything is fucked up,'
He then narrated her everything about the fight that had taken place between him, his Mother and best friend, Bunny.

She too had tears in her eyes when she said, Why are you doing this for me? Your Mom is right,'

That means I'm the only one who is wrong?'

You're not wrong. These stipulations and circumstances are just not good for us!'

What do you wish then?' he asked

It's never too late to make a correct decision. My life is also messed up and I don't wish to complicate your life because of me,'
He said nothing. Instead, he just kept looking at her shimmering image on the laptop screen.

Harshil, are you listening?' she asked.

Yes,'

Let's just end it,'

That's why we started, didn't we?'

Oh hello, I never made a commitment. Be practical,' You really want this to end? Please don't. You know I Love you and I know you also Love me,'

She interrupted and said, Stop! Control your emotions. Getting separated from each other is the best thing for both of us. You're a free soul, I am also a free soul. You're free to follow your life, instead of that stipulation step by my Dad. I respect you a lot for making so much of efforts, but for that, if you start losing you own relations than that's a wrong thing. I will never allow that to happen. It's over, Harshil.'

As soon as she said so, Harshil could sense the tears coming out from her eyes. But she was extremely strong not to show any emotions on her face.

How could you do this?' Harshil asked.
She looked down and replied, I told you I had dated many guys, and I was only serious about Riyan. I'm glad I wasn't serious about you, because I knew our little togetherness would end up nowhere,'

She further responded, If I'm in your life, then there will get nothing except needless suffering,'

Accepted, but don't leave me,' he pleaded.

Okay. Fine, I won't.' she said with a smile on her face.

She just glanced endlessly on the screen without saying a word. So he asked her, What

happened?' Isn't it strange?'

No,'

You're the only guy to whom I've looked back again after giving up.' she said. All those guys in past had told me to trust them, but you're the only one who ensured my trust even without gaining it,'

I'm yours,' Harshil said.

I'm yours too,' she said giving him a flying kiss, and that kiss was the beginning of something substantial.

She suddenly asked him, Have you ever done a phone sex?'

No. Not even in my dreams!'

Oh shut up. That's not carried out in the
dreams,' Then guide me!'
She immediately stood up and placed her webcam in such
a way that her whole body was seen on the screen by
Harshil.

What are you doing?' he asked.
Instead of retorting, she untied her hair, and said,
Complete me!'

This left Harshil confused? Was that a sexual appeal or
sexual plea? Whatever! Who cared? He was damn excited.

She slowly moved her hands over her backless kurti,
and untied it completely from behind. To tease him more,
she turned around so that he could see her gorgeous back.
After giving him a little tease, she came back towards the
webcam and said, That was just to make your mood.'

You almost had my virginity,' he said.

She blinked her eyes, but soon after her looks
changed. What happened?'

Although today I did this, don't expect it to happen
every time. That relationship is the worst relationship
where a girl feels that she's nobody except a slut for his
guy,'

Don't worry. I swear that it will only happen at your
wish,'

That's why I love you,' she said, gaily.

Now tell me that when are you coming back from
Kolkata? I'm missing you.'

Miss me more. Still a few more days are
left,' Okay. I'll be waiting,'

Even I'll be waiting for you,' she said flashing her
eyes and disconnected the video call.

Minutes later, she messaged Harshil to go home, and resolve the matter with his Mother and his best friend, Bunny.

Convincing someone is the toughest task in an Indian culture.

If you want to do a love marriage; you've to convince your parents first even before convincing the girl.If you want good marks in viva; you've to convince your professor by giving the answers up to his satisfaction.

In conclusion, convincing is always done in the interest of something positive. And what would be more convincing other than asking for the forgiveness of your mistake?

Bunny was wrong when he addressed Manshita with a tag of bitch, but Harshil should have not slapped his best buddy. Mrs. Rama was right in her reserved way when she put forward her opinion, but rather than exaggerating, Harshil could have managed that situation with care.

Taking all that into consideration, he went back to his home, and entered inside his Mother's room.

Maa…' he said.

She didn't look at him.

I'm sorry. That's all I wanted to say,'

Ladies are sometimes so rigid. She kept ignoring him. Finally, after a long pause she responded, You're sorry for what?'

For my misbehavior,' he said.

The point stays the same. Choose me or choose her,'

Why are you doing this?' he asked as tears ran down through his gills.

I know you love her. I don't know, but yeah, possibly she loves you too but you have no future together. You cannot see that, but I can see,'

Maa…When I'm with her, I'm happy. I smile,' he said

Look it's very simple, Harshil. You can be the reason of her smile, but you can't keep her smiling. At present she is happy with you, but she can't stay happy with you. Our financial factor will affect both of you. Why can't you understand such a simple thing?'

Why don't you understand this one simple fact — we love each other. We will be there for each other in dark and light. What on the earth is stopping you?'

I'm not against your love. I will be the happiest person to see you both settled, but that's the matter — you're not settled, and her father is expecting way too much from us,'

Mom, she loves me!'

Does she really love you? Wait, let's test,' she said. She brought the cell phone and said, Call her and ask,'

Ask what?'

If she really loves, then is she ready to leave her parents and marry you?'

She placed the cell phone in his hand.

Keep it on the loud speaker. If she agrees, I have no issue,' she said.

You were never like this. Why are you being so rude?' Are you calling her or not?'

I talked with her before I came here. You know, when I told her about our fight, for an instant, she ended up everything and motivated me to live for you. She advised me to prefer you ahead of her,' he said. Fine, I'll call her and ask whatever you said. But I'm sure about one thing — she respects you more than she loves me. What else do you want?'

Mrs. Rama didn't say anything for a moment.

I'm just making one thing clear—I'll only marry Manshita. I don't know how, but yes, that day you'll smile,' This time she smiled and said, Of course I'll smile, because I know that nothing can happen unless you're a millionaire,'

I never expected you to blow me down. You were my strength!'

And I never expected that you would prefer a girl ahead of us,'

What do you want?'

You'll have to choose, Harshil.' she said.

Then I choose you,' he said immediately. Fine. So forget her.'

No. I'm doing one justice to myself. I'm leaving this house for nine months!'

Shut up!'

Now that's final. You jot your decisions, so now this is my choice. And don't worry, if I go no where, I'll return and do as you say. But If I end up becoming a millionaire, I'll still hold your hand and say, I love you,'

How could you love her so much?'

Like the same way in which you still love my Father. You love him so much that you still talk to him. It was you, who made me realize that love never sees the presence, it just sees the person.'

She said, Okay! Today, I will not stop you. If you want to leave this house to dispose of something, then you're free to go. But till then remember—you're alone,'

I've been fighting against this loneliness since I was a kid.' he said. If I don't show up against this millionaire challenge, then I'll end up fighting with my emptiness. In

either of the way I've to fight. Let me fight.'
She was blank. She didn't know what to say.

Till the present moment, you were never alone. You had my support and his support too.'

Who's support?'

'Bunny,' she replied.

The things are not the same now,'
She opened her drawer and took out one envelope and handed over to him. Today you've not slapped him, you've killed him. He was always there for you. Even today to bear your slap.'

Harshil hesitantly opened the envelope and escorted the piece of paper which read —

Harshil,

I never imagined a girl would influence our friendship someday. So weak was our bond that it had to end because I told you the truth?

However, it's your life. So you have your own decisions. But still, Manshita is not the correct decision of your life.
She will end you. She will destroy you and leave you like you hell. I hope that you realize this fact soon. I'll be waiting for the day when my original friend comes back to me, as well as my aunty.

As a best friend, I don't want to be a hindrance in your life. Neither do I want you to lose or me to win. I know, I may be wrong regarding Manshita, but just remember — the day you'll marry her; I'll be the first person to dance like a drunkard in your baarat'.

Parth has prepared that fake ID card for IIT-Delhi. I couldn't attach it in this envelop, so I've kept it over the photo of your dad.

This is perilous task. I know you've always done tough things in your life, but still I request you to not do this for her. Her family's demand is not worth this risk.

We always shed tears for the thing we really love. Yes, I've seen you slipping those tears when you were deprived from entering IIT by the difference of just two marks.

I've seen your tears, but more than that, I've made you smile. So as your best buddy, it will always hurt me when some stupid girl and her family will be the reason to ruin that smile, which I carved after so many efforts.

I may appear unjust. I might be wrong. I might sound self-centered, but please - never hate me! You may get Manshita. She will love you anyway, but you will never find someone who didn't care about his self respect, just for your smile.

Bunny

LET ME SEE YOU LIKE THERE IS NO TOMMOROW

Old Delhi is one of the busiest railway stations in India. You are deemed fortunate if you even find a place to sit on the self attested chairs on the platform.

It had been such a long wait, but finally Manshita was returning from Kolkata. Harshil wanted to greet her personally, so he didn't give her a hint about his arrival on the station. As soon as the whistle of *Kalka Mail* was heard, he went to the location where her AC chair car bogie was proposed to halt.

For a moment when he shifted his attention; he saw one familiar face. He was the same small kid which followed them. The kid stared at Harshil with some sort of expectation. Those innocent eyes reflected the spirit that he too had been waiting for someone's arrival.

To sustain so long without Manshita proved to be a resilient phase for Harshil. He saw her walking out of the coach and said in his mind, Let me just see you like there is no tomorrow...'

However, he wanted to surprise her. So he wrapped his face by a white cloth and approached her in disguise of a coolie.

Madamji, can I help you? You won't be able to carry so much of luggage,'

Haan... As if *tera baap laya Kolkata sey idar tak!*' she responded in a rude tone.

Why are you so rude to the strangers?' he drawled.

What?'

That mentioning of ―Father‖ pinched him like a needle. He disclosed his face and said, Not everyone in this world is blessed to have a Father.'

She was shamefaced on seeing the actual person behind the wrapped face. She placed her palm on her lips and said in a conciliatory manner, Hey, I'm sorry. Do you think I could ever say that to you?'

You shouldn't say like that to anyone. You never know what's going on in someone's life,'

She gently placed her luggage on the ground, and then, she just opened her arms for him—to get submerged in the warmth of her hug. All the passengers on the platform kept gazing at them. Seeing the typical Indian behavior, Harshil felt vague. He said, Manshita, people are looking at us,'

I don't care. At present no one can separate us from this hug,'

But….'

Shhhhh!'

She brought her lips close to his stirrups and hummed, I'm very fortunate for these few moments together.Let's look at each other closely to our hearts' content. We never know if the fate will ever bestow this opportunity on us again. Or, we may never have such a chance in this lifetime. So don't care about anyone and come, embrace me because I don't know if such a beautiful moment will come again or not.'

She took all the emotions out of his body. He too whispered in her ears, Please come close because I may not see you again and again. Please let me cry over in your arms now because I am not sure whether the tears of love will flow again or not. Embrace me in your arms now because I don't know if such a beautiful moment will come again or not.'

She wiped off his eyes and said, I'm sorry! You came here to surprise me and I spoiled your mood by my rude attitude,'

You need not say sorry. Every single time when I meet you, I feel like I must have taken a rebirth to be there for you,'

You're so captivating,' she said.

That tells how fascinating you're to have captivated a captivator,' he replied.

I haven't captivated a captivator. I'm a captive of your tranquillity,' she said. Your love makes me feel at the top of this world,' she tacked on.

Not my love, it's our love!'

But I always feel that you're afraid of something. You can't even control your tears,' she said.

No one has ever taught me to control my tears. I used to assure if my Mother was sleeping or not, but no one cared about my sleep. Every night, I used silently cry beneath my pillow, but no one came to even offer a glass of water. I had to conclude that tears are sour in taste, and that's how I slept,'
She then kissed his cheeks and said, I love you,'

Suddenly?' he asked with a sort of pun.

Shut up! I really do. If a girl like me can say that she loves you, then trust me, any girl can stay happy with you,'

I don't want any girl. I only want you,' he said and saw her advancing towards the auto rickshaw stand.

Why to prefer auto? I'll drop you.' Harshil said.

No man, leave it. Dad won't like,'

Don't tell me that your parents aren't aware of the fact that we meet?'

Actually!' she responded biting her lips.

Fuck!' he exclaimed.

It will happen one day for sure,'

What will happen?'

The fuck,' she responded with a shy smile.

Like a decent guy, he put her luggage in the auto and said, I need to tell you many things,'

Even I've to tell you many things,' she said. As they were again getting indulged into the conversation, the auto driver gave a queer look as he was getting late. Harshil realize that such body language from the auto driver would enrage Manshita more. So he said, Hey, calm down. This time, don't show the middle finger.'

She laughed and got seated inside. Harshil touched her soft smooth hands and said, Take Care,'

—Where will I sleep tonight? Where will I live now?‖— Such thoughts were moving around his mind as he was about to depart for his office.

Some from behind came and kissed Harshil on his neck. To his surprise, it was Manshita.

What happened? Go! Your auto is waiting for you,' Harshil said.

She looked at the auto-rickshaw driver and said in loud tone, Fuck off!'

Hearing an abuse from a girl is always an insult for any guy. The auto-rickshaw driver immediately left.

Hey, why did you abuse him?' Harshil asked her. My anger always ends up in a form of an abuse,' Do you abuse frequently?'

Oh Fuck! That sound's like—do you smoke frequently? Come on, man! There's nothing bad in abusing. You feel awesome when you lift this middle finger of your wrist and randomly point it towards someone,' she said showing the gestures of the same.

That too regardless of anyone's fault?'

You will never understand this bitchy attitude. Abusing and fighting with random strangers is the only source of my time pass,'
Harshil had no clues about what to say.

She smiled and said, It seems that you've done no *pagalpanti* in your life,'

You're right. I've lived very ordinary life,' he said. She held his hand and said, Come. I'll show you how it is done.'

See took him near a tea stall outside the station and said, Let's have some fun. You just wait and watch my *pagalpanti*,'

Manshita, this is not a right place. I mean look at the way these guys are gawking you,' Harshil said.

You've still not seen the real Manshita. She knows how to tackle such wastes and drive to their extremities,'

As she went near the tea stall, the loafers who were standing there and sipping the tea glanced at her sexy figure. One guy from that group gave her a smile, and she too did the same in return.

Bhaiyaji, two cups of tea please,' she said.

Madam, you seem to be a single person then why two cups?' commented the guy who initially gave her a smile.

Who asked you to concern about me?' she said bluntly.

Relax madam! I said that very politely. You can answer me in a low tone,' the guy said.

I'm not answerable to you Mister...' she argued.

The guy forwarded his hand and said, My name is Hridant. I study in Delhi University,'

Dude, did I ask?'

Looking at her bold actions, one guy from the group whispered in Hridant's ears, Brother, her nature is just like her,'

Exactly, super hot!' shouted Hridant and gave hifi's to his fellows.

If you have balls like me, then say it on my face,'

Fortunately we don't have, but we always wish for such... you know...' commented Hridant in scornful way.

Actually you have balls, but they are like your thinking—Small. That's why they are hiding beneath your manhood,' she said in a loud tone, and that was enough to create a little crowd.

Hridant angrily pointed his index finger and said, You're crossing your limits,'

Ah, I see! Now when this crowd is staring at you; you're feeling insecure. But for a single second you didn't think how insecure any girl would feel when she has to make her way from the guys like you,'

Enough. Shut up!' said Hridant in loud tone.

Just remember that if I know the actual position of your balls, I also how to put nuts dead on your face,'

The mob turned up to cheer her. Even Harshil was applauding in her admiration. Hridant had turned red and felt embarrassed.

I'm not being a feminist, but see, this is the respect that every girl wants form the society. But Mister Hridant, you just deserve only one respect and that respect comes from the bottom of my heart and ends in form of my middle finger,' she said as she led her middle finger at the apex of his eyes.

The crowd gathered was truly enjoying the show. Before the things would go more acute, Harshil went there and told to Manshita, *Pagal*! Let's go,'

Hridant angrily stared at Harshil. He later turned his eyes towards Manshita and said in a low tone, You've humiliated me; I'll see you one day.'

Before Manshita could express anything further, Harshil took her aside and asked, Girl, have you gone mad?'

When there is smoke, I'm always around to burn it down,'

Seriously,'

I'm a certified A+ Bitch,' she said.

Will you do the same with me if we ever have arguments in future?' Harshil asked.

May be, or may be not,' she winked.

You were supposed to reach you home, weren't you?' Harshil said.

That was just to test you. I wanted to know your reaction when I rejected the proposal of your lift,'

You don't need to test me. Just trust me,'

I trust you,' she said. You know, generally if a guy has good nature, a girl will fall for him. Surprisingly, I find this thing very strange in our case,'

How?' he asked.

I'm falling for you, but that's not because of your nature. It's your character that drives me off for you, and you win my trust over there itself,' she said.

You're the first and the last girl in my life,'
She laughed and replied, Even Riyan said the same! But he had endless nights of fun behind my back,'

Life has surely cheated on me, but I've never been cheated in relationship. So I don't know how that feels,'

Forever Love, never ending promises, and imaginary intimacy — When you devote all this to the person you love then you start assuming you've nothing to lose. But when the same person shows his middle finger and cheats upon you; you end up with nothing except regret, and that regret is very hard to digest. It swallows the good people around you, and develops the feeling of hatred for the term called *love*,'

I'm not like him,' he said. I'm rubbing my ass off to complete your Dad's challenge,'

What if it doesn't happen?'

It's tough, but if you're there with me, it will happen for sure,' he said.

She sat behind and Harshil drove towards her home. During the entire journey, she crossed her arms over his waist and calmly placed her head upon his shoulders.

Wait. Stop, stop, stop!' she exclaimed.

Why? Your house is inside this lane,' said Harshil applying the brakes.

My society members are bit orthodox. They already made a story out of me and my trainer Viveek. If they see us together, they will make a story out of us too,'

Harshil shook his head and asked, Why are we born in India?'

Wow! This is really nice. Whenever there is a cricket match;
you guys will scream and put statuses everywhere like —
Come on India. And when there are little
contradictions around, you will always curse — Why India?'

Manshita really knew how to shut anyone's mouth!
But still Harshil smiled because his bitchy girl had much
more understanding and patriotic feeling for her country.

I'm sorry! It's not that I don't love my country,' he
said.

There where you're wrong — It's OUR country,'

Manshita, I need to tell you something very
important,' he said in the context of the whole incident
that had happened between him and his Mother. He
wanted to tell her that he had no shelter.
As he was about to say, her cell phone chimed.

Fuck! Dad is yelling. Someone made a story out of us.
Don't worry, we will meet soon,' she said and began to run.
However, she stopped in the middle and again came back.

I forgot to give you something,' she said as she
fetched for something in her purse. She placed the
identical yellow colored smiley ball in his hand. Harshil
smiled and asked, Again?'

I felt very special today. You really surprised me
when you came to the railway station to receive me. The
way you saw my anger at the tea stall, and the way you
chased a smile on my face when I again revisited my past
in front of you. This sponge ball is the symbol of the smile
which you lavished upon me today,' she acknowledged
and left because she was getting late.

Harshil kept looking at her and murmured, I have no
shelter, just for your smile!'

While Harshil was working at the office, his colleague came and told him that someone was searching for him downstairs. He immediately rushed down.

I had been waiting for you since long,' said a familiar voice from behind.

When Harshil looked at that person, he realized that it was none other than Parth, the same guy who had fixed the fake ID of IIT-Delhi.

What are you doing here?' Harshil asked him furiously.

Relax! You must be surprised at how I found your office address, right?'

No! I'm not surprised. I'm cognizant of the fact that you have information of your clients, but I'm surprised to see you here, all of a sudden,'

Dear Harshil, Bunny gave me the token, and I did the work for you. Now I'm here for the full cash payment,'

Oh yes! So you want

money?' Yes, exactly,'

At present I don't have that much money to make your full cash payment,'

Listen, I do very simple business. Once I complete the work, I need the remaining cash,'

I'm not running away. Let me get my salary by end of this month; I'll pay you,'

It's not about me, Harshil. I'm not the single one who has done this work for you. There is a secret agency that has undertaken this task, and now they are asking for money. If you continue to delay, the things might get messed up and it won't go in your favor,'

But seriously, at present I don't have that much of money,'

Why are you still working here?'

What do you mean by that?' Harshil asked.

Parth laughed.

What wrong?'

Going into the placement cell of IIT will be full of uncertainty. If you're caught, legal actions will be taken against you. So in that case, your house, your working place, everything that is linked with you will come into the consideration. Do you wish that?'

After hearing those words, Harshil was abruptly lost in his reflections. Moments later he asked Parth, What should I do?'

I can give you one practical solution—Give resignation,'

That's not possible. Where will I work if I'm rejected from IIT?'

But if you're caught, then everything linked with you will be in question. One act from you can trouble your family, friends, and the firm, for which you're working,'

Harshil's facial expressions were enough to say that he was stuck.

Don't think too much. Just give your resignation and take your salary. I'll meet you tonight at this same place with a hope that my payment will not be delayed anymore,' Parth said with a smile on his face.

Okay,' Harshil said with a glum face. You'll get your money tonight.'

That's excellent. Love is magical. It can make you do anything. After seeing you, I also believe in love,'

I'm glad that someone has learnt something from me,' Harshil said.

RELATIONSHIPS HAVE AN END,
LOVE NO END

Sir, I need to tell you something,' he said as he was standing inside the cabin of his boss, Mr. Neel.

Harshil, I was about to call you,' Mr. Neel said.

Me?'

Yes. I had recently checked the working statistics of my staff, and I found that you've worked overtime on number of occasions,'

Sir, the situation demanded the same from someone. So I had to step in,'

But now the situation wants you to more effective,'

Harshil was perplexed. Looking at his changed body language, Mr. Neel said, Man, I'm saying that you've been promoted,'

He was completely strangled after hearing that. For a moment, he forgot everything and enjoyed that moment of ecstasy, but soon the reality faded away the delight from his face.

Harshil, it seems you're not happy,' Mr. Neel said. Sir,

I'm not someone who has had years of experience
in your office. Then why am I promoted so early?' Harshil asked.

I'm not only your boss, but also the overseer of this place. Being a leader, I know everything about the strengths and weaknesses of my employees. I know that the ones, who are experienced, always try to bully the workload on juniors. Now since your hand is high, go and do the right thing.'

Harshil accumulated all the strength and said, I can't work for you, sir.'

What do you mean by that?' Mr. Neel asked roughly. Harshil felt humiliated. His head was down as he said, Sir, I'm quitting,'

Is that the reward you're giving me for my affection towards you?'

Please, don't think like that. This place has given me everything,' Harshil said.

And you're going away from it,'

Sometimes, life puts us in such a situation where we are not only left to compete against this world, but also with ourselves,'

What do you mean?'

If I had not to fight against this entire world; I would have never left this place. But for the first time in life, I'm competing against my own self. And for that, I can't risk the people who are allied with me!'

No need to give so much of explanation. You can simply say you're leaving because someone is offering you more salary,'

It's not the case yet,' Harshil said.

Well, whatever! You can give your resignation letter, and leave!' asserted Mr. Neel with no objection.

I'm sorry, sir. If it's possible, then please do forgive me.'

Mr. Neel affectionately moved his hand over Harshil's head and said, 'No hard feelings. Before building such a large empire I was an ordinary guy—just like you. A guy that had so many dreams, number of fantasies which were surrounded by the pressure of expectations from the society, and no proper road to set off for my dreams,

Then where did you go?' Harshil asked.

I never thought about that. Thinking would have never helped me to reach here. I just went on the path where my impatience led me,'

Will I make it?' Harshil asked.

I'll only tell you one thing — if you've really chosen to face your own self then just run away. Run so fast that this present you, which is full of doubts is left far behind. Run so fast that if anyone attempts to stop you, then you shouldn't stop, but the person holding you should fall down. If your dream is your limit, then reach at such a peak where you are on the top and you could see your dream turn into the reality,'

And what if I fail?'

Then the doors of this office are always open for guys like you,'

Those few influential words from his boss gave him Fatherly bliss. A Father is like a guide. He is the only person in this world who would carry his child on his shoulders and still teach him how to face this cruel world alone till the last breath.

It's not in everyone's reach to show their importance like a shining sun in the day sky. But there is always a second option in life. If we wish to show our importance, just as the moon which is often seen clearly in the dark sky, then we should know moon is not visible during the daylight.

Daylight suggests the leisure time. We need to sacrifice and work for our day, in order to shine at the night.

Big dreams require big sacrifices too.

Harshil was unaware of this fact until he took the challenge for becoming a millionaire. He knew that once if he was ready to do some big sacrifice for this dream, then no one could stop him from shining like a moon in the dark sky.

In the earlier phase of his life, he wanted to shine like a sun, but he didn't know that *a person only succeeds in the aura created by him, not the circumstances!*

It's true that all are not fortunate enough to achieve their dreams. But everyone is capable to work for the situation given in their hands, and it would surely take us somewhere. If not our destiny, then may be the road to our new destiny.

☺

After leaving the job, Harshil was at such a point in his life where everything broke him down. But that's where his love for Manshita strengthened him.

According to his Mother, he should have left Manshita. But how could he explain her about the infinite energy which Manshita's love had put in him to fight against this world? Harshil settled the payment with Parth.

After that he was waiting for Manshita at the garden near her residence. She had one peculiar habit. She always used to bite her lips upside down. So when Harshil saw Manshita, he too started to bite his lips.

She laughed and said, I usually do that, but why are you copying me?'

When you love someone immensely; you fall in love with the things they do,' he said.

You could have used a better pickup line,'

You're my equilibrium!' he said as he fondled her in his arms.

She whispered in his ears, What is equilibrium?'

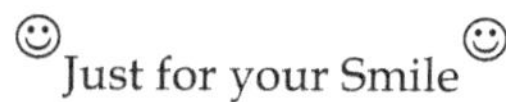Just for your Smile   Baman Tadiwala

In chemistry, whenever the rate of forward reaction equals to the rate of reverse reaction, then things become stable and such a condition is called equilibrium. Same way, I feel that forward rate of my love corresponds to the reverse rate of your love, and so I'm equilibrium whenever you're there with me,' he said.

Don't love me so much. I'm not that good,' she said. Forgot? I'm a bitch,' she added.

My bitch!' he said and kissed her temple.

The last time when I was at this place, I was with Riyan, and everything just happened in the darkness of the night sky,' she said with a sort of regret in her tone.

Harshil clung to her chin and said, Every time when I try to come close to you; you always remember him,'

Because just like I've touched your heart; he also touched my heart, and then my body,'

It's okay,' he said and got divorced from her arms.

We can't be physical till we marry. I'm sorry,' she said.

Fair enough,' he said.

This time she held his chin and said, But that doesn't mean that I don't love you,'

You're body is your temple, I don't want the lust. I want you,'

I love you, Harshil! I solemnly do,' she said and slipped in his arms.

What is love?
At that immediate moment, Harshil got the answer of this question. Love is respect. Nothing else!
That's the reason there was still a smile on his face even when she refused for any intimacy.

It really doesn't bother you?' she asked

But what?'
That I'm not a virgin,'
He smiled and replied, Haven't you heard that
song?' Which one?'
I don't care who you are?
Where you're from?
What you did?
As long as you love me.....' he sung.
So yeah, it doesn't hinder me,' he added.
I seriously wish to meet Rama aunty now, and thank
her for nurturing you in such a sweet way,'
Harshil said nothing. The image of his mother
flashed in front of his eyes.
Come on, let's go! I want to meet your Mom,'

Hey! Are you okay?' assured Manshita when she him
numb. He narrated her everything. He was out of his
emotions when he described about the fight that had
taken place between him and his best friend, Bunny.
Manshita got the biggest shock of her life when she heard
about the gamble which he would play for her at the IIT.
Each act of Harshil physically attracted Manshita towards
him. She tried her best to control her feelings, but finally
she gave up on seeing his dedication for her. She came
closer and kissed on the tip of his nose.
Wow! That was cute,' he said.
It was the month of winter. The water droplets were
frozen like tiny crystals over the grass surface. She brushed
her index finger on the cold grass; seized the dewdrops on its
tip and rubbed the chilled water on his lips.

Manshita…..' said Harshil as she sought to position her lips over his mouth.

Before he could complete his say; she vigorously removed his jacket. Harshil had no clues — whether to go one step ahead, or stop there itself. However, he too got induced in her seduction. In the feeling of this enigma, he too removed her jacket. She kissed his lips, and that gave him a prickling sensation inside his tummy.

Manshita closed her eyes, and it seemed as if she expected something more from him. At the other hand, Harshil had never been in such a situation before. He brought his lips near her eyes and said, Manshitaaaa…'

She turned her face, and passionately steadied her lips over his lips. She refrained from moving back, and then their salivary glands automatically began their own exercise. They kissed passionately, pumping out extra amount of salvia to make its way into their mouths by the means of erotic tongue twist.

Complete me today,' she whispered, and again got engaged in his lips

But we are in the park,'

Shhhh!'

Hormonal excitement ran down through his body. Those feelings stimulated him as he lifted her, and showing a fraction of reflex to his action, she wrapped her knees around his thighs. He inserted his hands in her back, and gave a smooch kiss on the very epicenter of her neck.

Ummmmm…..' she moaned.

He kissed every corner of her neck. This increased the intensity of her moans, and every single time when it reached its climax; he chewed her lips and suppressed the moans within him.

In the excitement, his fingers went inside her skirt. He felt the wetness of her love because it had widened every cell of her body. She fetched her hands into his jeans, opened its button, and began to stroke.

Uhhhh! I love you' he said as he felt the utmost happiness.

After that, both of them hugged and lied under the canopy of stars. She accustomed her head on his chest. Both of them wanted to say something, but they didn't say a word.

When Harshil was about to sleep, she asked him, Why did you leave your house? You didn't think for a single second about the lady who nurtured you without the support of your Dad?'

I love her so much, but she is against us,' he said.

I may add a meaning to your life, but she is the one who gave you the life,' she said.

She paused for a moment and then asked, Why are you doing this?'

Just for your smile.' he said.

You are doing for my smile, isn't

it?' Yea!'

Just like you, even your mother had to face everything. You were never alone. Bearing all the pains, she still carved a smile of her face. Do you know why?'

Why?'

Just for your smile!' she replied.

Harshil felt ashamed. He said nothing.

You love me, and you also love her,' she said Your love for me can be defined, but you can never define her love. It's just way too pure,'

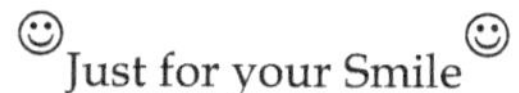
Just for your Smile   Baman Tadiwala

I'm sorry, Manshita. Forgive me,' he said with pity eyes.

If you cannot adore your Mother's wish, then you could never love me!' she claimed.

I really love you,'

If you love me, then you will do as I say,' she said. He was speechless. She looked into his eyes and said, Tomorrow will be the most important day of our life. You will go to IIT. Fate of our relationship hangs there itself,'

What do you mean by that?'

It's very simple, Harshil. I can't see the differences between you and your loved ones because of me. So tomorrow, if you get that big hefty job, then I'm yours forever, and if you don't, then you will live your life like you lived earlier,'

Why are you doing this to me?'

Because a girl like me will come and go away from our life, but your Mother won't. She is the only one, and she needs to be ensured. A person can live without food, but not without water. Same way, you can survive without me, but not without your friendship with Bunny,'

Okay, if you want it that way — I accept,' he said. But you will never find someone who will love you as much as I do,'

Don't worry about me. Heart is only broken once,' she said looking the other way.

Then why are you building this distance between us?'

Love has no distance, but yes, there is surely a need of distance in our love story,'

That day Harshil sensed one more fact about the girls.

He realized that if you wrinkle her lips to 180 degrees and make her smile, then she changes your life like never before to 360 degrees. Love is sometimes suppressed due to the boundaries created by the situation. Harshil was ready to hold her hand and defeat every possible hindrance that would come in their way. While at the other hand, Manshita preferred to surrender to those boundaries.

Do you wish to know one dark secret of my life?' Which secret?' he asked.

I don't have my mother,' she said.
Harshil looked confused.

She is not there in this world,'

What are you saying? Then who was that lady that day?'

She is my step-mother. There were complications at the time of my birth, but still my mother preferred to bring me in this world without even worrying about her own life. She passed away within a few minutes after my birth,'

She added, People say that as soon as I was born, she held me in her arms, and the joy on her face was worth seeing. That one moment before the death provided her the happiness of life time,'

Harshil immediately cuddled her and kissed her forehead. He said, I love you, Manshita. I never knew that we both are the shadow of the same tree. I had to live without my Father, and you had to live without your Mother,'

She pointed her finger towards the sky and said, Every night I try to find her in this sky, but I don't see her,'

Because she is not there in this sky,' he replied.

But people say that when someone passes away, they

become a star,'

That's true, but your Mother took a new life, as soon as she died after giving you birth. She revived her life in you, so that she could live freely and most importantly — she could exist in you! Your actions, your words, your smile, your tears, all that are ultimately her reflection. You will never find her as a star because she flows in your veins,'

She kissed his forehead and said, You're lucky to have your Mother. It's true we won't be left alone. At some point of life, we're going to hold someone's hand. But till then, nothing will replace that love which our parents gave us by holding our tiny fingers, and teaching us how to walk,' she said.

Harshil said, The day we will realize the real meaning of the love, we will miss their love but it won't come back again. Because parents are eternal, and they stay forever in our little infinity of love,'

She took out the photo of her Mother and just hugged it until she felt relieved. No one in this world can take the place of parents in one's life. Parental love is the only relation we do not choose on our own. It's a gifted relationship — that's why it is pure! Other relations which we choose on our own risk always have an expiry date.

Harshil saw the photo of Manshita's Mother and exclaimed, Wow! She looks like you!'

No! She was more beautiful. I'm a bad bitch who could abuse and shut down guy, but she was a divine lady,'

Well, now I understood. Just like my Mother is everything for me; your Father is everything for you after your Mother's demise. That's the reason he wants you to live like a queen, and marry to the one who is millionaire,'

Exactly! But that doesn't mean you should go against your loved ones because of this stipulation,' she said.

Tomorrow I will try my luck for the final time at the IIT. If I'm lucky, then we will continue, else *hum hai rahi pyar ke, fir milenge chalte chalte,'*

Will it be easy to forget me?' she asked.

Let me also face the break up!' he said with a

smile. *Pagal!* This isn't break up,'

In my opinion, this is break up,'

If it was break up, then do you think I would still sleep in your arms like this?'

I don't know. I have never faced break up. So I have no idea,'

She winked and said, You don't even need to know. A guy like you only deserves to be loved,'

Form a girl like you,'

I'll always love you. Even if we marry someone else, we will still stay close to each other,' she said

Extramarital affair?' Harshil asked.

No.' she said. If I get a son, his name will be Harshil. If you get a daughter, name her as Manshita. This way we won't miss each other,'

It's never about the time which two people spent together. It's all about those moments which they cherish to stay intact.

May be that's the reason we may fall for the person whom we have never seen because they accept our dark side which we don't wish to see.

Love never happens. It just grows. Relationships have end, but love has no end. Trust can be broken, but the bondage cannot be broken. Anyone can promise, but hardly anyone can do something — just for your smile!

☺ ☺ ☺

LITTLE SPERM,
BUT NOT SO LITTLE EXPECTATIONS

That day finally arrived and he was all set to enter the campus of IIT-DELHI. It was the most important day of his life and he was nervous. But more than that, he was worried about his Mother.

Life always gives a second chance, but there is always a slight fear when we create our own chance.

Do your best; I'm always with you,' Manshita said and kissed his forehead.

I'm missing something!'

What are you missing?' she asked.

Maa....' he said peering into her eyes. He was perplexed.

Moments later he said, That picture is coming in front of my eyes when I first appeared for the IIT exam. That day she had blessed me. Today I'm missing her,'

Then why are you stopping yourself to seek her blessings today?' she asked.

She won't bless me,'

Why? Stop making assumptions,' she said, and saying nothing more, she held his hand and directed him towards his house

She is your mother. No reason in this world can stop her from loving you. So go inside and take her blessings,' Manshita said.

At this hour she must be sleeping,' he said.

Just touch her feet and come back. After all this, I know you will be only hers,'

Won't you accompany me inside?'

Of course!' she said and encircled his palm.

Harshil straight away rushed in his Mother's room and saw that she was sleeping peacefully. She had covered her whole body by the means of a blanket to keep her warm from the cold windy weather of Delhi. Harshil sat down on his knees and touched his Mother's feet.

It was a delusion but suddenly those words ringed inside his ears – —It's the time to show everyone you're the best in the world.‖

Stop, don't do that. Let her sleep.' Manshita said as he was about to uncover the blanket. She instantly seized Harshil's hand and drew him out of the room. Expressions on her face had swiftly aged. She was mute.

What's wrong dude?' he asked her.

All of a sudden she started to wind her lips. Seconds later she immediately carved a smile on her face and said, Nothing. I'm just little worried about you,'

I feel hopeful after seeing her,'

She kept smiling and said, I think now you should go to IIT,'

And where will you go?'

I'm waiting here,' she said with a naive expression.

He placed his both the wreaths on her shoulders and said, Everything will go will.'

She looked down and replied, Things won't be the same. It's not that easy, Harshil,'

☺

IIT - DELHI

The gamble of creating fake identity card turned
into his favor as no one stopped Harshil from entering
inside the enormous campus of IIT. But the real task was
to get inside the placement cell for the interview.
He went to the administrative office and asked to the
peon sitting there, Can I get the form for job interview?'

At the first sight, the peon examined him properly
from top to the bottom. This look from the peon
chagrined goosebumps inside his body.

Which year?' the peon asked roughly.

Of course 4th year,' Harshil countered confidently. I

thought you're a postgraduate student,'
Rather than saying anything further, he preferred to
remain silent.

Which branch?' the peon questioned.

Harshil closed his eyes and said, Mechanical!'
Peon handed over the form to him. It felt as if he
was holding his dream in his hands.

Oh, Hello, This form is not free. Give me
one hundred rupees,' the peon shouted.

One hundred rupees?'

It's the cost of this form,' peon said.

You mean to say that this piece of paper costs
one hundred rupees?'

Placement fees are separate. It's not involved in
this,' Harshil shrugged his head and threw the money on
his table.

Sab Ch****** atte hai yaha...' the peon said as he
took the money.

☺

On examining the form carefully, he figured out that companies such as Google, Infosys, Aditya Birla group, Tata motors, TCS, and Microsoft would recruit fresher men this year.

Fuck!' he exclaimed when he saw one column in the form which asked for the final academic marks along with the SPI and CPI grades. He got stuck because he had not created a fake mark sheet which would act as a proof for his SPI and CPI grading.

Harshil went near the desk where regular IITians were simultaneously filling more than one form with extravagant zeal. Yes, after four years of rubbing their ass, they were obviously expecting a job with hefty salary package.

On examining each and every student minutely, Harshil observed one South Indian guy who appeared little nervous. *Strike the iron when it is hot.* Harshil took the opportunity of that nervousness and went near him.

A pale white shirt, grey pant, and a traditional white *tikka* on head was enough to prove the appearance of a pure Tamilian.

Vanakamm, anna' Harshil said with a hope that the guy would be impressed by his introductory Tamil gesture, and wow! That really worked as that guy grinned and asked, Are you from Chennai?'

No, I'm a local boy. But I know littlr Tamil,'

Oh!' the guy said and changed his facial expression as he figured out that Harshil was making a jest out of him.

Actually I've one doubt. Is it important to have the mark sheet as a record for our SPI and CPI grades?' Harshil asked.

We haven't got our mark sheets yet. So why would

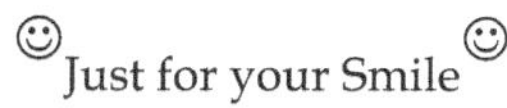

they ask?'

Seriously?'

Aiyyo… Are you a dumb or what? We always get the mark sheet at the end of the session, and the present session is not yet over,'

So what do I've to mention here?' Harshil asked. Your average grading out of ten which you've scored till now,'

So if there is a slight error, do they cross check?'

They will definitely cross check if your grading is above eight,'

Why so?'

Aiyo, don't be foolish. Not everyone over here can score that much,'

This brought a relief to Harshil as he jotted 6.5 pointers in the SPI and CPI grading column of the form.

Harshil looked at the guy and said, My name is Harshil, and I'm from Mechanical,'

Well, I'm Murli Durraiswamy, Computer Engineering department,'

Murli suspiciously looked at Harshil and asked, Were you ever detained?'

Harshil smiled and replied, Yes anna, two times!'

Aiyo!!! Then I should call you anna. You're my senior,'

Murli then looked over Harshil's form and asked, Anna, can I suggest you something?'
Harshil nodded.

Don't apply for big E's like Microsoft and Google,'

Why? You're applying for the same, isn't it?' The recruiters from such companies cross check everything. I think you don't have the previous years mark sheet, so if your grades are checked, you might get in some trouble. I suggest you to apply for some Indian companies first.' Murli said.

Why was Murtli suggesting Harshil to change his preferences? May be because of the hefty competition amongst the IITians? Or perhaps he was telling the truth. Whatever!

What are you thinking anna, change the choice,' Murli repeated.

Harshil smiled and replied, You're right. Being an Indian, I should first apply for Indian companies.'

Harshil quickly changed his choices and submitted the form to one another peon who was sitting there. The job of that peon was to prepare a list in descending order of the SPI and CPI grading. This meant that Harshil's name would be somewhere in between.

It was actually a knotty situation because most of the colleges are well known for recruiting the ones at the bottom of the list. Meanwhile toppers have to pass through dangerous questions from the recruiters, and then the leftovers in the middle get only one thing—Ghanta!
In no time the list was pinned on the board and as expected his name was somewhere in the middle.

What's your number?' Murli asked him.
28,'

Good luck, anna. Wish me the same,'
Harshil carved a fake smile and said, Good luck,
Murli. Just rock the stage,'

Today I will rock it.'

Murli was the last candidate to apply for the Google. No Sooner did he go inside the placement cell, moments later, a loud screaming noise of a lady was heard.

Harshil saw Murli rushing out from the placement cell. He was breathless. Seeing that, Harshil got hold of him and asked, What happened? Why are you running?'

Murli took him aside and said, A big problem has taken place,'

Why? How was your interview?'

Fantastic! Until that lady screamed,'

Yah I wanted to know why did she scream?' Interview was awesome. Everything went well until the lady assured me to be honest with my answers, and soon after she asked me to illustrate the hardest thing for the man,'

So what's wrong in that?'
Murli covered his manhood and said, I think I've highlighted a wrong thing,'

☺

Finally, after all the gamble and fun with Murli, it was now Harshil's turn to give an interview in front of the recruiters. Since the college days, he had mugged up all the basics regarding how to impress the opposite person in an interview. Remembering the words from his Mother, he entered inside the placement cell——You're the best in this world.‖

He thought that there would be barely two or three recruiters inside, but it was like a game of two halves when he saw a panel full of seven recruiters and each of them looked intimidating.

Our confidence level is not under a question until we pretend. Harshil had a smile on the face but his legs were shivering.

Please be seated,' said the lady who was the representative of the entire panel. Her name was Annavi.

After the formal greetings, the lady from the panel asked him, Google, Microsoft, and many big companies are here today. Why did you prefer us?'

Without any fear Harshil responded, The first face which a new born baby would see in this world is the face of his Mother. Later on, it sees other faces. That's the reason I wish to work for an Indian company first,

Or may be because of just 6.5 pointers?' He broadened his smile and said, If a person of five point someone can become a best-selling author, then six point five can at least work for you,' All of them laughed.

It was becoming a friendly environment until the junior most recruiter suddenly asked him from no where, Friendship, loyalty, trust and faithfulness are always tested in adversity; else anyone can be friendly at the coffee table. Do you think this statement is applicable in the corporate world? What are your views?'

Harshil looked at him and confidently said, To be honest, I'm not so good person at the coffee table. May be that's why I never had a girlfriend. But yes, in corporate world coffee table is the most significant place. It's the place from where wonders can happen,'

Can you explain?'

Imagine that I'm working for your company, and if I had to do some sort of settlement deal with a person of other firm who is quite whimsical, Then instead of talking to him directly, I would take him to some rich coffee shop. That would be a perfect place to make any settlement of deal. It's assumed that a person who represents a big post never gets hyper at social places such as coffee shops,'

Will you pay his bill?'

Of course! Once the deal will be finalized the same person will turn into my money multiplier, so why will I hesitate to pay his bill?'

All of them were convinced by his answer and they noted something on the data sheet. The lady recruiter smiled and asked, You said you never had a girlfriend. Why?'

I thought this was a technical interview,' Well

first you can answer specific questions,' I think

I'm not really good when it comes to communicate with girls,' he answered.

If we recruit you, and place you in the team full of girls, then how will you cope up with them?'

Ma'am, I said I can't communicate freely with a girls, but I can deal with ladies. My female colleagues will the ladies recruited by you, bearing some responsibilities and I love to work with someone who is responsible,'

I'm also a girl. Don't you think I'm responsible to recruit you?'

According to me, a girl can never be as responsible as a lady. And yes, you're sitting here to hire men, not a guy. For me you're a responsible lady because I'm not a guy, I'm a man!'

Again they noted something on the data sheet. After few moments, one gentleman from the panel asked, Can you tell me one common thing Mr. Harshil?'

Sure, sir.'

If you're from IIT, then generally you're paid more. Is it a myth or a reality?'

Harshil was stuck for a moment, but he confidently

replied, Yes, sir. It's a beautiful myth called reality,'

That's what I'm asking you, why it's so?'

Expectations!' he exclaimed and closed his eyes.

Expectations?' the gentleman questioned back. We

expect to get a job with high salary package,'

He laughed and said, Mr. Harshil, that's what I'm
asking you. Why do you expect?'

Harshil took a deep breath and replied, Sperm!'
Other recruiters who were sitting silently and enjoying
the ragging suddenly remarked, Excuse me!'

Sir, the journey of this term *expectation* arises from our
sperm itself. By mistake if the sperm is fertilized, its
producers start expecting whether it will be a damsel or a
chap? By mistake if it is damsel, she is expected to follow the
bonds of our society. Luckily if it is a chap, he is expected to
fulfill the bonds of our society. In this way, one follows those
bonds, and other fulfills it. Why so? Because it's expected
from the society. Even if you're smart and intelligent, but still
if you can't score well, then no one will help you to reach IIT.
So again it is expected from society that you should score
well. Further by mistake, if you score well and enter IIT, you
are expected to do good in each and every semester in order
to get noticed from the mob that includes thousands of
sparkled minds. So, I can conclude that the expectations
which were enforced on me since I was a sperm has brought
me here today in front of you. For the first time in twenty two
years this sperm is expecting something for him, rather than
the society. So what's wrong if we expect a good salary?'

All the recruiters again marked something on the
data sheet.

Now questions from your curriculum: Why a 4-Stoke Engine is used in airplane?'

Because 4-Stoke engine can only be used,' Harshil replied.

The lady recruiter laughed and asked, But why?' It's like that only, ma'am,' replied Harshil coldly. Did you clear your exams like that? You have no technical information concerning the subjects of your field,' she said in a high tone.

She thought Harshil was a virgin who had an immense knowledge about the engines. But very little did she perceive that he had studied about the same before six years, and engineers only study one night prior to their exam and forget the content as soon as possible!

Harshil said, Well to be honest, I never paid attention in the class when this topic was taught,'

The senior most recruiter adjusted his spectacles and said, Why?'

I knew I would never deal with planes, so why would I waste my energy and time learning about its mechanism,'

Wow! It's a curse to believe that you're an engineer from IIT.' the senior recruiter said bluntly. Again the same question was humming in Harshil's mind — how to make them understand that he was not from IIT?

Harshil accumulated some courage and said, Engineer is an engineer, sir. IIT is a mere tag given to separate the quality,'

Do you consider yourself in that quality?'

Never,' he said. It's not limited to me, but every student standing outside is not a quality engineer,'

How can you say that?'

You see that's our problem, sir. If we cannot answer a simple question related to our curriculum, we are not considered as a quality engineer. According to me, a quality engineer is the one who excels after being recruited. He has an opportunity to apply his knowledge for the firm which has shown the faith and thus recruited him,'

The recruiters were quality engineers. One of them said, Half knowledge of engineering is dangerous, kid,'

Sorry, I don't agree with you. Half knowledge is never dangerous. It's far better than having no knowledge,' Again all of them noted something in the data sheet.

One final question: Depict any one thing which dishonors you as an Indian?' the beautiful lady recruiter asked.

His eyebrows suddenly lit up. The blood began to run through his veins. He sharply looked at her and asked, Can I have the freedom to ask something?'

All of them nodded.

Where are you currently sitting?' Harshil asked. In the placement cell,' they replied

Where is this placement cell situated?' IIT,'

In which IIT?' Harshil questioned.

IIT-Delhi.'

Cool. Now where is Delhi?'

In India!' they whispered silently.

You represent a Multinational Indian company. You can go anywhere in the world and recruit anyone. If you find India so bad, then what are you doing here? I agree that there are many issues in my country. People are still poor, illiteracy prevails, and corruption is at its zenith,'

So do these factors dishonor you as an Indian?'

No! Being Indian you're asking me such a question dishonors me,'

I respect your feelings, Mr. Harshil. Though it was important for us to know what you feel about your country,'

Excuse me sir, it's never my country. It's our country?' said Harshil.

Well, let's be honest. In India population is high, and good job vacancies are too less,'

Each and every *Sardar* of India is not a Mechanical Engineer, but still he is the best mechanic of his area. Each and every South Indian, who is an engineer, is not working in a reputed firm, but still he is the best mathematics teacher of his area. Not every Gujarati can spend lacks of rupees to study Business in some reputed Business school. Instead, he learns all that by himself and still has the guts to be the richest person in this country. Sometimes a person running a Momo shop in a small corner of any North-Eastern city of India has more turnover than a person doing black collar job. Do these facts dishonor you as an India? Don't know about you, but make me proud,'

Sorry Mr. Harshil, you're very blunt. I understand that you love India, so you cannot hear anything against it. But what will you do if the same situation happens when you work for us? You won't be hearing flattering words every time. Looking at the position; you've to even face bitterness and still remain calm,' they said. Well, we wanted to check your anxiety level,'

I'm sorry for that, but I still don't back off from my statement,'

Why?'

Beacuse they were meant for my country,' he said. The tears ran down through his eyes as he continued, I came here for my Mother. It was her dream to see me in IIT. But her shadow was limited, until I left my house and came here. What still kept me going was one another Mother– the very land on which we are currently sitting. My Mother has only given me the birth, but this land of India has fostered me. When I was a kid, my own Mother satiated my thirst through her milk. Now when I'm an adult; water quenches my thirst, and I drink that water from my Motherland. How can it dishonor me? You may believe that gravity is an observable fact, and as a cause everything on the Earth falls down. Even tears fall down, but a person who gives those tears moves ahead. Where is the gravity? Every single time when I've cried, this Indian land has absorbed my tears in its soil. How can this karma dishonor me as an Indian sir?'

Meanwhile, someone entered from behind and said in a vigorous tone, Stop all this!'

Police?' said the lady as she saw three stout men. On seeing the highly fermented look on their faces, Harshil shivered.

This is it.' said Harshil in his mind as he saw them approaching towards him. The policemen angrily kicked the chair, and as a result, Harshil fell flat on ground.

On seeing this barbarous behavior from the policemen, the recruiters got tensed. The lady recruiter literally screamed. The fire alarm chimed and everybody rushed inside the placement cell.

What's all this? Why are you beating him?' asked the junior most recruiter.

The Policemen held Harshil's collar as he hoisted him

from the floor and said, This boy is a fraudster. He has cheated under the name of this illustrious establishment,'

What? How is that possible? He is from IIT, right?'

No. Can't you figure that out from his age?' the Policemen questioned back.

The junior recruiter then scanned his eyes over the application form and said, He has failed twice, so that's reasonable,'

The policemen said to the recruiters, Don't be a hindrance in our work. We have solid evidence against this guy which will expose his act in flashes,'

What's the proof?' the lady recruiter asked.

The policemen snatched the ID card from Harshil's neck.

Check this ID card and scan it,' said the policemen as he handed over the card to the peon to check the same. Moments later, the peon came inside and said, Sirji, this is a fake ID card. It doesn't match to our data system.' There was an absolute silence. The next thing which transpired was no where in his dreams. His both the hands were locked by a means of handcuffs. This was a brutal sign of a culprit. Meanwhile, the press and the whole media bustled outside the placement cell. Two of the Policemen came and clasped his arm from both the sides so that he couldn't escape.

I've one request,' he said to the Policemen. Please cover my face. If my Mother sees me, she will die,'

It's too late. You could have thought about the same before doing such a thing,' said the Policemen. However on his repeated request, the Policemen agreed and he was allowed to tie a rag of cloth just to cover his face. While they were arresting him, he stopped for a moment and looked at the recruiters. He lifted his hand, which were now sealed by handcuffs and said, Sir, this thing dishonors me as an Indian.'

He continued as he said, I was not born in any SC/ST/OBC family, so I couldn't get any reservation. This fact dishonors me as an India. Before six years, I was left short by only two marks to study in this college. This thing dishonors me as an Indian. I could never try it again. This nature dishonors me as an India. I love everyone around me, but today, I've letdown my own people. This fact dishonors me as an India,'

The policemen then dragged him out of the placement cell, and the whole media just thundered over him. They captured him, and broadcasted the live headlines. They constantly questioned about his name, but the Policemen dragged them off and said, Very soon we shall release an official statement.'

As he sat in the Police van, he uncovered his face. Huge crowd had assembled outside the college. Despite of such a rush, his eyes got stuck to one kid. Yes, again he was the same kid who constantly followed him and Manshita. Harshil was sure about that kid because like always there was a sketchbook and a pencil in his hand.

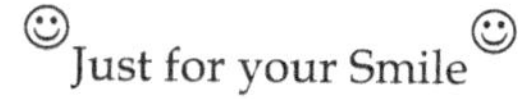

LOST IN THE LUST,
REDISCOVERED IN THE HANGOVER

He was not made for happiness, So he hid all the sorrows of his life. Success was never meant for him, So he hugged all defeats of his life. He was always a defeated person, but now — he was finished! If love was easy, life was not!

If life was easy, love was not!

If both were easy, he was not!

Harshil was behind the bars. One big mistake had taken away everything from him.

Tell me everything in detail. Why did you do this?' asked the inspector as he threatened him.

For my Mother, for my Love,' he responded with low breathes.

Shut up! I don't want an emotional drama. Else we know the ways to make you reveal the truth,'

I'm saying the truth,' he responded.

He is saying the truth,' said a common voice from behind.

On hearing that voice, Harshil got little hope, and he said, Wait, that's Parth!'

Who is Parth? He is Mr. Siddharth. He claims to identify you,' said the inspector.

That's nonsense. His name is Parth, not Siddharth,'

Sir, if you don't mind, can I talk with Harshil for a few minutes in peace?' Parth requested.

Inspector left the cell and locked both of them from outside to talk. After the inspector covered a far distance, Parth looked at him and said, I'm Parth for you, but not for everybody,'

Harshil wiped off his wet eyes and said, How did this happen?'

Someone has lodged a complaint against you on account of cheating with IIT,'

Only three people in my life know this

thing,' Who are they?'

That's You, Bunny and Manshita,'

Who is Manshita?' Parth asked.

You always asked me for whom I was doing all

this?' Yes?'

So she is the one,'

Was she aware of this thing?'

Yes. She knows everything. You and Bunny were unaware about my action today, but she was the only one who knew it!'

Parth consolidated Harshil as he said, 'Friend, don't take me the other way. If she is the only one who knew this, then the things are pretty obvious,'

What do you mean?'

Umm...I mean, I'm not sure, but I think she has lodged a complaint against you,'

Shut up! She would never do this. Instead, she had supported me for this thing,'

Be little logical. Things are pretty clear. Use your mind. This love and all is just a myth, nothing else,'

It's not a myth,'

It is a myth. It's okay if you we love someone truly from our heart, but why do we forget to use our brain?'

It's a coincidence, Parth.'

Coincidence?'

Our love was a coincidence. I never knew Manshita. She was living a different life. Perhaps a happy life, I must say!'

So it's an arranged marriage,

right?' Right!'

Then how did this love happen?'

As I said, it's a coincidence,'

Gosh! I'll never understand this thing. I mean to say why so many of efforts for an arranged marriage? It's completely out of my head. It's not a coincidence dude, it's a pure myth,'

I don't care. What I know is that I love her, and she also loves me back in the same way,' he said. It's easy to love someone, but seeking out the same love from the same person in return is a coincidence. A pure coincidence which happens only with the fortunate people. I'm extremely blessed to be part of this coincidence,' he added.

If she loves you, then she should be the first person to be here,'

She must be taking care of my Mother,' Harshil said, but deep inside he wasn't sure about it.

The Inspector suddenly came, and opened the lock. Your time is up,' he said.

Parth looked at the Inspector and asked, Sir, can you tell us about the person who has lodged a report against Harshil,'

We received a phone call came. I can't give you any

further details,'

Parth again asked in very deliberate manner, Was the phone call made by a lady or a man?'

Lady!' exclaimed the Inspector.

What!' Harshil shouted in disbelief.

Parth warned Harshil as he said, These officers are little old-fashioned. They won't tolerate if you raise your voice,' He further said, The call was made by some lady, and Manshita was the only girl who knew about this thing. The figures are very simple, my friend,'
Parth left, and Harshil was again locked alone inside the chamber. However, after some time, he thought that Manshita could never be the reason behind his current situation. There was surely someone else.

Sirji...' he said as he called the inspector who was standing outside the chamber.

What happened?'

Please get me out of here,' Harshil begged.

That's not in my hand. Let the jury decide,'

Please don't say like that. I'm not a terrorist. Neither I've robed or killed someone. I just went to a place which was rightfully mine before a few years,'

There is only one way for your
escape,' Which is that way?'

On the bail,' he said. 'Someone has to pay the bail.'

When the things will become normal, she will come and take me out of here,' Harshil thought.

☺

Many questions were rimming inside his mind.
Did he really want her at such a big cost?
Would she really appreciate his sacrifice?
Why did he do so much for her?

May be, there was only one answer at that instance in his mind–Just for your smile!' he said envisioning her.

But on the other hand, what if she was the solitary reason behind all this? We often say: we trust someone more than we trust ourselves. But if we forget to trust ourselves, then how could we trust anybody else?

Time would certainly crack the whole mystery, and that was the only hope he had.

☺

More than a month had passed, but she hadn't come for his rescue. Every single day, he tried to convince his heart that she was not the reason behind his situation. But her absence forced him to conclude that she never really loved him.

After one month

Harshil, come out. You're now free,' said the Jailer.

Is that really true? Harshil asked hesitantly.

The Jailer opened the lock, and after a month or so, Harshil walked outside the chamber.

How did this happen? I thought I'll always stay here,'

Annavi madam,' he said. 'She is the reason behind your rescue,' replied the Jailer.

Annavi? Who is she?' Harshil asked.

Before he could inquire anything further, he was asked to sign the papers of his bail.

But who is Annavi? I don't know her,' he said.

I'm Annavi,' said a humble voice from behind.

Harshil looked back to make out and he was utterly floored.

Annavi was one of those recruiters who were there that day

at IIT. She was the same person to have asked him what dishonored him as an Indian but why did she turn up for his rescue?

Don't worry,' she said consoling him. Just sign these papers. You'll be free from here,' she added.
After signing those bail papers, both of them went outside. Harshil couldn't resist himself and said, Ma'am…'

She abruptly cut him and told, First of all stop addressing me as ma'am. You're done with all those formalities at IIT. Call me by my name. I'm Annavi,'

Why did you rescue me?'

Is the reason necessary?'

Yes!'

Then listen: How could I see such a brilliant person behind the bars? You impressed me a lot in the interview but why did you cheat?' she asked him.

When no one had come for his rescue, this lady had arrived as a blessing for him. So without giving a second thought he decided to tell her everything.

So you can see that my luck never favors me,' Harshil said concluding the entire matter.

Sometimes luck may not like us, because hard work and determination may end up loving us. I'm so impressed by seeing your efforts towards your love,' she said.

But she didn't come for my rescue. I guess she doesn't love me,' he said.

Sometimes love is just not enough. I also loved someone, but he could never be mine. As in reality; I never really wanted him,' Aanavi said confidently. Then what did you want?'

Success! I'm a person who adores journey rather than the destination. Love is a permanent destination, but at the other hand, success is not a destination. It's a journey. I've seen nights, where I had no one except my shadow, who taught me that how dark yet beautiful my own soul is!' she said.

She added, I've seen people come and go; relationships die and grow. I've realized the secret of successful survival.'

What is that secret?'

The secret is: we all have to flow alone in the river called life.' she said.

Harshil was lost in her words.

Well, forget that. I've got something that can make it up for you,' she said.

I'm confused,' he said.

Well, I know you're confused. Accommodate inside my car,' she said.

Where are you leading me?'

You want the job that will make you a millionaire, don't you?' she questioned.

Definitely,' he said and sat inside her car.

Annavi took him to her bungalow which was far away from the city. She gave him the keys, and told him to open the door. While he was doing so, she untied her pony tailed hair and threw the buckle on the floor. She looked at him, and started to play with her loosened hair.

What are you looking at?' she asked with a shy smile on her face.

He looked down and said, Nothing.'

This reminded him of the scene when he saw Manshita for the very first time. She had also untied her hair and flapped them in the similar manner. As they both entered inside the house, Harshil's heart started to beat because it was something more than *just a cozy place.*

Is this your house?' he asked Annavi.

Yes. I made it with my own money,' she said.

It's mesmerizing. Every brick depicts your hard work,' he said.

Someday you will also have such a lavishing house,' Her house was not less than a five star hotel. From private gym to swimming pool; it almost had everything.

She went near the bar desk, exactly opposite to the main hall and asked Harshil, Do you drink?'

Yes, but…' he said, feeling shy.

She brought a huge tray comprised of two empty glasses, ice bucket and a bottle of vodka. He looked at her and said, I have never tried vodka,'

Do you want this job? Yes or No?' she asked.

Yes!'

How bad?'

Whatever it takes,' he said firmly as she dropped the chill ice cubes into the glass filled with colorless alcohol. She rose and sat beside him and spoke, Before I officially recruit you for our firm, we have to carry out this last sort of physical interview,'

Physical interview? What is that?' he asked

I want to know how effective your senses are in the hangover of vodka.' she said extending her own glass of vodka. After that, Annavi offered him seven more shots of vodka, which were plentiful to take him in an intense hangover. His eyes went down, and all of a sudden, his throat started to burn.

How does it feel?' she said as she placed her hand on

his chest.

He couldn't as his throat was dead. To awake him, she sprinkled concentrated soda on his face, but still it was not enough to shake him.

Fine!' she exclaimed 'Just feel the heaven,' she added as she seized his hands and tied them off.

He somehow muttered, What are you doing?'

Oh yes! You're in your senses. This is good; you will enjoy,' she said.

Annavi, Can you tell me what's going on?' he wanted to know as gradually he appeared to recognize the cause.

She held his chin, parted a tender kiss on his lips and said, Nothing,'

Wait, we can't do this!' he said and dragged her out. Come on, Harshil. Show me your enigma,' I can't cheat her. I love her,' he said.

You won't be given such a wondrous opportunity. Tonight just forget her.' Harshil decided to move, but since his stakes and paws remained joined, he couldn't act.

Annavi, you're not doing a proper thing,' he said. She towed him, sat down on his lap, and injected a drug inside his body. This immediately made him calm. After that, she untied him, and took him inside her bedroom.

Harshil had no intimation about what was flowing through his mind. Hormones were excited to act, but at the same time he was tensed.

As they entered inside the bedroom, she jumped over his shoulders, and kissed his neck from behind. He grabbed her, and bit her ear lobs — provoking a slight moan. His other hand came up around her arms and he fondled her breasts. After a good and thorough kneading, he grabbed the opening in her blouse and opened the buttons, leaving her bare stomach exposed. She felt his teeth gently down on the back of her ear as his fingers rolled around in her belly button. She felt heaven as her legs shrilled. His fingers sliced inside her thigh, under her skirt till it finally reached the very epicenter of her virginity. He squeezed it till the drops of her juice trickled out.

She could resist as she left her legs open and allowed him to full access her sexuality. By now, she was sopping wet, her panties were down at his knees and his hands scoured the soft moist curve of her tender slit.

Manshita…' Harshil muttered.

Annavi kissed his forehead and said, Yes. I'm your love,'

She was shaking almost uncontrollably. That sound of unbuckling the belt and unzipping his jeans were clear indications for the intimacy.

My tongue is stuck out for you,' she said in an enticing manner.

Soon she felt the first taste of his spur. Then she slowly wiped the head of his strength around her lips, spread the saliva-coated knob on her cheeks and eyelids. Within moments, she ripped off all the remaining bonds, and now the two naked bodies got stuck to each other with deep compassion.

Manshita, don't do this. We're yet to get married,' Harshil said.

I'm Annavi. I'm your love for tonight,'
Moments later, she again injected something in his veins.

I love you Manshita, but why are you giving me so much of pain,' he said. He could barely see anything. She tied his wrists. He desperately wanted to jump and run away, but it was not feasible!

Please, let me suck you!' she implored as now she was over him. She reached down between his legs and pushed the head of his boner against her opening. She rubbed it back and forth across her lips. He tried to strangle the last attempt to resist, but alas he was a man — he couldn't restrain.

Oh God, Please stop it!' Harshil begged.

But the deepest and most terrible part of the night set in when Harshil started to enjoy. Her legs squeezed against his thighs. Her resistance aroused him as he rose to the occasion. He couldn't prevent! Harder he drove off her, the deeper she ached to be picked.

Those orgasmic swells swirled around her vaginal clench. The trigger turned on, and like a huge volt of light, the orgasm of high force swept out like a gum and bore on their bodies. She screamed — just to anguish her fantasies like never before.

Fuck!' she exclaimed and again injected something through his veins.

☺

The next day

As soon he opened his eyes, he was astounded on learning his appearance. His joints were aching and his hand was bandaged. Soon, he realized that he was naked.

He looked up and saw Annavi. She was gazing at the window and enjoying her coffee.

Take it easy,' she said.

What's all this, Annavi? Where are my clothes?'

She kissed his neck, but this time he dragged her away and said, Have you lost it?'

Last night, we made love!' she said.

Utter nonsense. I was with Manshita, not with you,'

119

Harshil, last night you thought that I was Manshita,'
Harshil was shattered. Tears flowed down from his eyes
as he gazed her.

Why did you do so and what did you get from it?' he
asked her.

I did this for you. You'll be a rich man

soon,' But now I can't look in her eyes,'
Annavi reminded him and said, If she loved you, then
why didn't she turn up for your rescue?'

There must be some reason. I love her,'
She threw that coffee cup and said, Can't you see that I too
love you?'

You don't. I'm confused by your actions. If we really
love someone; we never make out with them, especially in
an extreme hangover condition. There is sex in love, but
love is not sex,' he said as he wore his shirt.

So you're leaving me after quenching your thirst last
night?' she said angrily.
Harshil preferred not to reply.

You can't leave me like this,' she screamed.

And you can do anything by injecting a drug inside
my body?'
She had nothing left to say after that response.

☺   ☺   ☺

LOVE IS A BITCH

He left her house and directly went to his own place. His eyes were desperate to see his two girls: Manshita and his dear Mother.

Maaa...' he shouted lustily as he entered inside the house. He went in her room; searched for her in every corner of the house, but she wasn't there. Before he could derive any conclusion, he saw her faint image near the staircase. She was standing there in the absolute darkness, and as a result; her shadow fell right over Harshil's face.

If we have done a wrong thing, then there is always a fear of facing our own parents.

Harshil had done a wrong thing. His legs trembled as he went towards her.

Mom,' he said from behind. She didn't utter a word.

Mom, I'm sorry! I should have told you,' he said. I left our house in anger. I'm sorry for not obeying your request. Do you have any idea how much have I missed you since that day?'

She was numb. She didn't react.

I know I've done a wrong thing, but I've realized my mistake. I promise, I'll never leave you alone,'

His words were still not enough to apprehend the trust within her.

I still remember those nights...' he said. There was a fixed silence. He continued saying, You fought with Dad's image for leaving us alone in such situation. You've the right to fight with me as well, but at least say something. I cannot afford to lose you. I love you maaa... please talk to me.'

Harshil,' said someone from behind.

Bunny!' he replied with a categorical blow on his face.

Bunny's eyes were filled with tears. Without saying a word, he embraced Harshil, and wept haphazardly over his shoulders. Harshil wiped off his tears and asked, Why are you crying?'

I'm sorry. I couldn't be there at the time you needed me the most,'

Bunny, stop crying! Droplets don't fit in your eyes,' Are you all right?' he affirmed Harshil.

No, I'm not. She is still not talking to me,' said Harshil and gazed at his Mother.

Aunty isn't here!' exclaimed Bunny in a remorseful tone.

But she was there,' Harshil claimed Bunny didn't respond.

Just a few seconds ago, she was there,' said Harshil with a shock beacuse this time when he searched for her, she wasn't there!

Mom....' he again shouted.

Bunny grabbed his wrist and said, Harshil....'

What?'

She is not with us,'

Then where did she go?'

Bunny closed his eyes, and again the tears poured out. These fissures were now repelling him. He again went inside her bedroom. This time his eyes fell shot to read when he saw his Mother's image was hanging alongside his Father's photo-frame.

Those shivering legs suddenly felt the effusion of blood streaming into them. The reality was in front of him. His Mother was no more. He lost his temperament and vigorously screamed. Bunny rushed inside the room and just like a true brother, he picked him up and kissed his forehead in solace.

Just a few moments ago, I felt as if I was talking to her asking for the mercy. How did this happen?' Harshil asked.

Do you recall the day when you came along with Manshita?'

Yes!'

On the very same day, aunty passed away peacefully in the sleep,'

She was sleeping.' Harshil said. Even Manshita didn't permit me to disturb her,'

Actually, Manshita had instantly figured it out. But she never wanted to break you as it was an important day of your life.'

Harshil recollected the ultimate sentence that Manshita had said to him that day——Things won't be the same. It's not that easy, Harshil.‖

An ocean flooded with the dignity of bearing so much of water never knew it would become a desert one day.

Such change had taken place in his life. When there is a grave regret in one's life, the question of living only looks like a sheer survival! In order to complete that stipulation set by Manshita's Father, Harshil had to leave his house, and ultimately at the end, he lost his own Mother.

He thought, she died as she couldn't bear the pain of separation from her son.

He said, Bunny, I can never forgive myself. I'm the one who killed her,'

It had to happen one day. It's said that nothing is more certain than death and nothing is more uncertain than life,'

I never gave the happiness which she deserved,' You were only the reason she used to get up early in the morning and live whole day—just for your smile!' And I did nothing for her smile,'

Actually, you did. Since you were not there during her funeral; I had to carry out all the rituals and I offered the fire on the pyre,' Bunny said. If a person dies happily, there is always a shinning glow on the face. Trust me, I found the same glow on her face, when I saw her for the last time on the pyre. You know, that glow on her face was due to the happiness you both shared during the togetherness of her life span,'

Bunny got up and brought something from inside. This urn contains remnants of your Mom,'

Harshil's hands got stiffed frozen as he took that cinerary urn from Bunny. He opened the urn, inserted his palm, and moved his fingers freely between the lumps of ashes. All he could feel was nothing more except peace! Each and every particle of her ashes silently symbolized only one thing to him——You're the best in this world.‖

It's a ritual to offer these ashes in the river Ganga,' Bunny said.

Not now,' replied Harshil and embraced the urn.

Why?'

She always said that I'm the best in this world. She will never rest in peace unless I prove I'm the best in this world!'

Materialistic achievement will not make you the best in this world,' Bunny said. To do something which can benefit the whole humanity will make you the best person in this world,'

How can I do that?'

I've watched each and every phase of your life. You've always done all things for someone's smile. You got good grades, just for your Mother's smile. You wanted to become a millionaire, just for Manshita's smile!' Bunny explained. What have you done for your own smile?'

Where is Manshita?'

Bunny took the urn from Harshil's hands and said, She has stepped down from this marriage,'

She cannot do that,' Harshil said with disbelief.

She can, and she did. I know, you'll hate her for this, but she was the only one who informed the Police about your act,'

For the first time in life; his heart was crushed because of some girl. *It hurts when the person we love the most becomes the reason of our suffering. But it hurts more when the same person is not even there to support us in our suffering.*

I want to meet her,'

Meeting her will simply hurt you more,' Bunny

said. I don't care; I want to meet her,'

Harshil...' Bunny said. Manshita is marrying someone else,'

A thin line of tear spilled down from Harshil's eyes. He sent her a text message asking her to meet for one last time.

☺

He was quietly sitting on the bench and waited for her to come. In this awe of silence; he didn't realize her presence as she sat beside him.

Congratulations! I heard that you're marrying someone else,' he said breaking the jinks of deep stillness. She looked at him without saying a word. She wanted to cry, but somehow she was strong.

Who is the guy?' he asked.

His name is Hridant. The same guy who encountered us that day at the railway station,'

So he was there in your life?'

Yeah,'

Then why did you love me?'

Because I wanted to,' she replied.

You always did what you wanted.'

There was a brief silence after that.

You never wanted to be someone's girl like that, your family always wanted a millionaire and now you're marrying a person like him?' he asked.

Surprises me as well,' she said with an innocent look. I think I will never accept that. It makes no sense to

me,'

It just happened,'

That's what I don't understand. What happened?' Few days after your Mother passed away; I just woke up one day, and I realized,'

Realized what?'

That I was never sure of with you,'

His eyes turned watery. He immediately looked the other way because he didn't want her to have a glimpse at his moist eyes. He chucked his throat and said, It sucks, Manshita. Realizing that every single thing that I believed about you, it sucks!'

What do you mean by that?'

All those shits like destiny, soul mates, true love and care. These all things are myth,'

Harshil got up and decided to leave, but she held his hand and said, 'Harshil, don't leave like that. You're still my best friend,'

You were right, Manshita. At every single step you were right,'

Really?' she asked and then she began to laugh hysterically.

Why are laughing? What's so funny?'
She had totally lost the control. She couldn't stop herself from laughing.

You're fucking crazy,' he said.

Well, it happened at the time when you were behind the bars. One day, I was waiting for my friends in some restaurant. Hridant accidentally comes up to me, and we discuss our lives,' she said. Now, he will soon become my husband,' she added.

Yeah, so?'

So what would have happened if I had been to shopping that day? It would have been totally different scenario if I went somewhere else for dinner? Imagine, what if he showed up a few minutes after my friend had arrived?' she said.

She placed her palm on his fingers and continued, Harshil, it was meant to happen. And as it was happening; I kept thinking that you were always right about love. It just wasn't me you were right about,'
He was speechless. As she took her hand away, he noticed an engagement ring affixed in her index finger. *If one single word is enough to make your day, then sometimes one single sentence is also enough to break your life.*

Well, before you go; I just need one last favor from your side,' Harshil said.

I'm sorry. We are just done with all the favors in our lives!' she said and began to walk.

He kept looking at her, but she never looked back.

Manshita…' he shouted, and she stopped for a moment.

Are you really happy with him?' he asked.

She just smiled and went away. After a few moments, he once again saw that kid. He was standing there with a sketchbook and a pencil in his palms.

Harshil went near him and said, It's surely not a coincidence. Why do you follow us?'

The kid didn't utter a single word. Harshil touched his sketchbook and asked if he could have a look at his sketches, but before he could see them, the kid refused and ran away.

☺

Bunny advised Harshil to go and apologize to Annavi for his abusive behavior.

Annavi,' he said as he got into her house.

She was amazed on seeing him.

I'm sorry for my behavior. I was disturbed,'

She hugged him and said, You need not to say sorry. Actually, I'm sorry to have done that without your concern,'

He made her sit and revealed each and every nook of his entire life.Tell me, after realizing all this are you still ready to even like me?'

She just smiled.

He laughed and said, Hah! I knew. Well, I should go.'

Harshil,' she said.

What?'

She tugged his cheeks and said, I'll be honest. Until the last night; I just liked you. Now, after learning your past and your dedication; I seriously respect you,'

How can you?'

You were in prison for more than a month and still you loved her like it was forever. During this entire phase, she didn't pour a single drop of love and you kept showering your love. How could you love someone so much?'

It's very simple. I believed that my all hopes were beneath her smile. When I saw her; I felt good. When I saw her smile; I felt more relieved. Yes, I loved her more than God,'

But what do you think about me?'

I don't know. But I'm here in front of you, isn't that enough?' She smiled and said, More than enough,'

Annavi, will you hire me?' he asked. I'm jobless.'

Of course,' she said. Well, I've one more idea. You will definitely love it!' she added.

And what is that?'

She gripped his fingers and said, Together we will work for your Mother's wish.'

I'm so scared to trust a girl again,'

I'm a woman,' she replied.

Making an eye contact she further said, And One more thing, I'll never force you to love me,'

But what about that love?' he asked purposely.

She smirked and said, For sure not in a hangover,'

Why?'

You were damn submissive,'

Are you serious? I never knew it,'

How would you? You were super high after a few shots of vodka. In every moan, rather than uttering my name, you were just saying — Manshita… Manshita…'

Now the things have changed. I'm sorry for that,' he said.

You can make it up for me. Tomorrow is my birthday. Since past few years I've celebrated this day alone. I'll be thrilled if you at least spend some hours with me,'

Why do you celebrate it alone? What about your parents?'

A tough question, but they don't exist for me,' I'm sorry?'

They don't love me. They just love their sons,' Misunderstandings, I see!'

Nah, it's a reality. They always wanted their sons to be ahead than me. I was only meant to be tied in the knots of society. So one fine day, I ran away and rest all you can see,'

Time changes everyone,' he said.

Time changes everyone, but if you try to change your daughter's wish as per what culture and society wants; she will only hate you. Let her be free. Let her walk in her own way. She will fall but I promise, she will create a new culture and a legacy which every single person would be proud of,'

Don't you ever miss them?'

I do.'

Have they ever tried to contact you?' he asked.

I don't know. My family occupies only one place in my life,' she said.

Which place?'

She took of out her cell phone and said, In my block list.'

☺

In the evening, both Harshil and Bunny decided to have beer at Hauz Khas Café. Bunny soaked in and said, I told you that Manshita is not the one for you, but you and your love...'

Love is a bitch,' Harshil responded.

Actually it's not. Annavi is rather better choice than Manshita. Don't forget, she's rich,'

Bunny, love must be a choice for you, but for me, it's an epitome to rejoice. I don't want to repeat the same mistake again with a different person.'

Just because you guys had an affinity in hangover; you consider her as your mistake?'

Bunny...'

Don't forget, she was the only one who came for your release. She was the one who hugged your sobs. Don't you realize this?'

I do, but that doesn't mean that we are something,'

I don't know, but I see something symbolic in you guys!'

What?'

You were introduced to Manshita by your Mother, and you instantly fell in love with her. After aunty left us, Aanavi was the only face you saw in your life, and she also likes you. Isn't that something meaningful and symbolic?'

Harshil looked at the other way and said, No!' Bunny got up and said, I'm not telling you to love her; I'm just telling you to follow —the Bunnyll trend,'

Bunny trend? Now what on the earth is that?'

In sequential order if I explain, an old trend was something like this: Meeting, Friendship, Love, and Sex. These days it's like: Sex, Love, Friendship, and Move on. Since in your case the first one has occurred; I would suggest you to follow the Bunnyǁ trend,' he said. It has only two stages: Sex and Friendship. In my opinion, if any girl can readily understand your friendship, then there is no need to make her understand your love,' he added.

Annavi only likes me. She doesn't love me,'

That's why she is perfect. She said what she felt. Manshita had pacified your heart by her words, but Annavi is a different girl. Manshita had to follow her family, but Annavi is someone who knows the value of your sentiments which are surely more important than money,'

What should I do then?' Harshil asked him like he was asking God.

As you said, tomorrow is her birthday. Let's make it special,'

But what can I do? I've no

idea,'I will tell you....'

And after that, Bunny said something which enlightened Harshil's heart and generated a strong desire to prepare Annavi's birthday surprise. After hearing Bunny's idea, Harshil realized this one plain fact—*There exist a few friends in our lives who surround us during some problem. They provide sets of advises and number of ways to get over from it, but they never help us to implement their own suggestion.*

Then there is one best friend like Bunny who not leads us to one simple advice, but also hangs there while we implement it.

Like any normal friend, Bunny never used the word—move on as he knew that this word would simply upset his best friend to a larger extent.

Sometimes we don't want to hear the word – move on.

All we want is a person who moves along with us during that phase.

☺   ☺   ☺

SURPRISE

He constantly looked over his watch, and when only three minutes were remaining for 12:00 am, he rung the doorbell.

Annavi, open the door,' he shouted as he knocked the door.

She opened the door, and she was flat surprised on seeing him at this point of hour. Harshil griped her fingers and told her not to say anything for a moment. As soon as the clock stuck 12; he cuddled her and whispered in her ears, Happy Birthday, Annavi!'

Oh my God, you could have wished the same on the call,' she said.

Why? Didn't you like this physical wish?'

No, it's not like that. I didn't expect. I'm shocked. Thank you so much,'

You can thank me later on because this is just the beginning,'

What do you mean?' she asked.

Before she could get any traces, he quickly covered her eyes by a means of silk *duppata* which was lying down on the sofa.

Hold my hand and move along with me,' he said.

Where are you taking me?' she asked as she held his hand.

☺

SURPRISE #1
12:10 am
(1st hour of surprise)

Will you tell me what's going on? What are we doing here on my terrace?' Annavi asked.

There are twenty-four hours in a day. Since it's your birthday, I want to make every hour of this day special,' he asked as he uncovered her eyes.

I'm still confused,' she said.

It's quite simple. At an interval of every one hour; I'll give you one surprise. This way, by the end of the day; I'll try to give you twenty-four such surprises,'

I can't believe,' she said giving him serious look.

Well, you can decide that later on,' he said, For the first five hours, let the nature wish you,' he

added. How will the nature wish me?'

There are five elements of nature: Air, Water, Fire, Wood, and Metal. Trust me, today these all elements will simultaneously wish you,'

Nature is natural, but nature wishing me? — That's unnatural,'

I will say happy birthday, and nature will write your name,' he replied

Okay. Then show me,'

Bunny was the mastermind behind all twenty-four surprises. Harshil had to only give a signal, and rest was all Bunny's show!

Fire will wish you first,' he said, Look at the sky,' She curiously looked up, and he roared, Happy Birthday…. Happy Birthday…. Happy Birthday… Happy Birthday…'

For an instant, nothing happened. She looked back to him and asked, What?'

Have patience. Nature is not under my control,' he said.

Suddenly Harshil saw that thing.

Hey Annavi, look,' he said pointing towards the sky. She looked up, and her eyes were stupefied by the yellow glow of those fire balloons. Minutes later, many such fire balloons were seen floating on the sky bed. She was pantomimed. But the actual plan was something different.

She looked at him and exclaimed, This is so beautiful!' And when she again looked at the sky, one strange phenomenon took place. The balloons arranged itself in form of letter A, followed by N, N, A, V and I respectively,'

Hey, what's happening?' she said as she felt little scared.

Don't be scared. It's not myth, nor is it a magic. It's just a little application of Mechanical Engineering,' he said.

He then came closer and whispered in her left ear, Happy Birthday…'

And the fire balloons completed his sentence by adjusting themselves upon the sky bed as— A…N…N…A…V…I

SURPRISE # 2

1:00 am

(2nd hour of surprise)

While they were on terrace; Bunny had arranged the second surprise inside her house. He again wrapped her eyes and took her downstairs.

Second element of nature is ready to wish you,' he said. The cloth was removed. This time she saw a huge fish aquarium with number of tiny fishes inside it.

Harshil quickly switched off the lights and whispered in her ears, Happy Birthday...'

And this time, the green radium letters jotted inside the aquarium glass along with the water gleamed —

A...N...N...A...V...I

SURPRISE #3
3:00 am
(3rd hour of surprise)

He then took her to a Neem tree outside her home.

Close your eyes again,' he said.

He continued, Trees are also living. They eat, drink, and breathe like us. What they can't do is abusing. Since they don't abuse, they are as innocent as newly born babies! We always adore the cuteness of small babies, and as it's your birthday today; I request you to adore this Neem tree,'

How can I adore it?' she asked.

You can just cuddle it. When we are sad, all we need is a hug. Trees are speechless, they demand nothing,'

As she embraced her arms around the wooden stem; he quickly arranged the dry leaves on the ground.

She peeked down and asked, What are you doing?'

Happy Birthday...' She was ecstatic when she saw those dry leaves arranged as —

A...N...N...A...V...I

SURPRISE #4
4:00 am
(4th hour of surprise)

Sit behind me,' he said as he started his bike

Where are you taking me?' she asked.

I'm driving towards the tallest building of this city,'

As they reached the place, they saw two security guards standing still near the gate. Annavi, take this!' he said.

Fuck! It's a pepper spray!' she exclaimed.

Fuck yes. They won't allow us to enter inside this building, and with this pepper spray in your hand; you know what to do.'

In order to get protection from an aftereffect of the spray, both of them covered their faces like a dacoit. As expected, the guards stopped them. Annavi immediately sprinkled the pepper spray. The guards fell down on their knees and began to sneeze virulently. Taking the advantage, they quickly rushed inside the lift and reached the terrace above 20th floor.

This is total *Pagalpanti*.' she said.

The expression on his face suddenly reversed when he heard the word — *Pagalpanti* It notified him of how Manshita had inspired him to do some *Pagalpanti* in his life.

Are you okay?' Annavi assured.

He diverted his mind and told to her, Our city looks so beautiful!'

In order to experience the real eccentricity of the cold winds, Annavi closed her eyes. I don't want you to close your eyes,'

She said, I've never experienced an early morning like

this before,'

Harshil caressed her from back and said, Happy birthday...'
She was lost. She sensed those cold breezy winds from all the directions.
A... N... N... A... V... I — was the only shrill she could feel inside her body.

☺

SURPRISE #5

5:00 am

(5th hour of surprise)

This is the final surprise from the Nature,' he said. Are you really up to twenty-four surprises?' Yes,'
I still can't believe. Please don't make me fall more and more towards you,' she said.

He placed his index finger on her lips and said, I'm not rich. I cannot buy you expensive gift like gold rings, bracelets and all. But I've got something more interesting,'
And what is that?'
Umm...Promise me that you won't laugh. It's actually a silly gift,' he said.
She agreed and he gave her a metal box and said, You can open it,'
She hurriedly opened the box. She couldn't control and ended up laughing. Hey, I told you not to laugh,'
I'm not laughing. It's just out of happiness. How can you be so cute?'
You like these rings?' he asked her. I know you will not wear it, but still I have tried.' he added.

139

I loved it,' she said. How did you make it?'

I had metal wires at my home. I only encircled it together, and studded these precious stones at the top like a cherry on the cake,'

She kissed one of the rings and exclaimed, This is so cute!'

I'm glad that you even regarded such a small thing,' he remarked.

It may be a small thing for you, but for me it's the biggest gift I've ever received,' she said.

What's so special about it?'

Your efforts!' she exclaimed. The efforts which you made by encircling these wires to stud these precious stones. I'll wear your efforts proudly. It will always remind me that someone spent a whole night making this for me,'

Just for your smile,' he murmured.

☺

SURPRISE #6

6:00 am

(6th hour of surprise)

After experiencing all the five elements of nature, he took her to one local café where Bunny had previously made preparations for the subsequent surprise.

As soon as she entered inside the café, she was overjoyed upon seeing her whole office staff. They had especially turned up to wish her at an early hour of the morning. These days cake cutting is followed by one more ritual, and that is to apply the cake icing all over the face.

As she was their boss, her employees were initially afraid. Harshil was the first one to take the initiative. He took a piece of a cake and smeared it over her face. He further signaled everyone to do the same. In no time, the whole cake was smeared over her face. She looked like a clown.

I'll kill you for this,' she screamed, with shy a blush on her face.

A small red cherry got stuck to nose. Harshil ate that cherry and said, Cake was tasty. Didn't you eat?'
`She acted like Aliya Bhatt when she said, *Basss… Ho gaya na Chutiyapa.'*

☺

SURPRISE #7

7:00 am

(7th hour of surprise)

What's next?' she asked him.

Now we are going to the destinations of faith,' he replied.

Which are those destinations?' she asked.

Wait and watch,'
We all are born naked, and a naked body has no religion.
Harshil wanted to deliver the same message to Annavi. He held her hand and took her inside the first destination of faith — Church. Prior to their entry, Bunny had again made all the arrangements inside the Church. Like a perfect man, Harshil wrapped his fingers around her palm and entered inside the premises of Christ.

Father, Today is her birthday. Please pray for her,' he said and went near the candle stand.

The Father of the Church looked at Annavi. Giving her an innocent smile he said, God bless you, my child,'

141

Sorry Father, but I've never experienced a thing called blessing in my life,' she replied.

Poor-old-Father took out his specks and said, But I see those blessing reaching you in some other form,'

In which form, Father?'

My child!' he exclaimed. Just turn around and see. They are reaching you in the form of love.'

She turned around and saw all the candles were burning under one name —

A...N...N...A...V...I

☺

SURPRISE #8
8:00 am
(8th hour of surprise)

You're a real guy, if you're the reason she smiles on her birthday. But you're a real man, if you can sustain that smile for every single minute of that day.

In those seven hours, the gleam of smile had doubled. She had never seen such a thing before. She was stunned when she saw that every flower vendor lying outside the pious *Hazrat Nizamuddin Dargah* sold the rose beds of only one word —

A...N...N...A...V...I

☺

SURPRISE #9
9:00 am
(9th hour of surprise)

Stop!' said the Pandit, as they were entering inside the temple. Ladies are not allowed to step inside this temple,'

Yea, I know.' Harshil responded.

Annavi looked at him and asked, Then why did you bring me?'

You cannot step inside, but you can see it with your eyes,' he said.

I didn't get you,'

Encircle your arms around my

neck,' What?'

Do as I say,' he said.

She encircled her arms over his neck.

I'll keep your word. She will not place her feet inside,' Harshil said to the Pandit. He then lifted her and said, She is already in my arms.'

Pandit didn't utter a word. He had never seen anything like that before.

Harshil looked into her eyes and said, This is a holy shrine. It's said that if we revolve around it for seven times, then all the wishes come true,'

I want to wish,' she said.

She was already there in his arms but then too he revolved around the holy shrine for seven times. He was sweating due to the heat outside the temple. He moved his hand over his head so that he could collect some sweat.

Happy birthday...' he whispered and wrote her name on the floor with those wet fingers.

In this world, money can be earned by efforts, but if you can put little sweat to make someone smile, then you're simply phenomenal. Harshil was surely becoming Mr.

Phenomenal for Annavi. The sun rays gradually evaporated her name, but it built a permanent soft corner for him inside her heart for rest of her life.

☺

SURPRISE #10

10:00 am

(10th hour of surprise)

I'm thirsty,' she said.

Don't worry. My next surprise will not only quench your thirst, but it will also quench your mood,' he said.

What do you wish to drink?' she asked.

Anything except vodka will do,' he replied remembering the incident of that night. They stopped at one coconut stall.

Six coconuts, please,' Harshil said. Why six?' Annavi asked.

Because it's your birthday,'

So what? I mean, I can't drink so much,'

Oh come on. Assume that it's revenge from my side,' Revenge?'

Yes. In front of those vigorous vodka shots that day,' She became little furious and said, If that's the case, I'm ready to drink all six coconuts,'

Oh! Seriously?' Harshil asked.

You've challenged an adventurous woman. Just wait and watch,'

First coconut… second coconut… third coconut, this way she drank the water from all the six coconuts.

Challenge completed!' she exclaimed.

Did you notice something?' he asked after a long

pause.

Tell fast, I want to go to the
washroom,' Fine, let's leave,' he said.

Oh fuck!' she exclaimed as she saw all those six
coconuts cut and carved in one word –

A...N...N...A...V...I
☺

SURPRISE #11
11:00 am
(11th hour of surprise)

*Each and every girl is a chocolate lover. And if she gets a guy who
is equally chocolaty, then the time spent together seems sweet.*

Relationships should be like a white chocolate — absolutely
pure. Love should be like a milk chocolate — absolutely
sweet. Trust should be like a dark chocolate — absolutely
deep. But in reality, all these feelings are like a nut
chocolate — absolutely mixed.

This box of chocolate is for you,' he said.
Her heart began to beat as she saw small pieces of diary
milk silk chocolate arranged in only one word —

A...N...N...A...V...I
☺

SURPRISE #12
12:00 pm
(12th hour of surprise)

*Action speaks louder than words, but when words speak along
with action, the person is definitely special.*

Harshil's only priority was to make Annavi feel special, but this time he wanted to do so by his words.

I've tried to write something for you,'
Annavi desperately opened that cute birthday card which read —

A true relationship is like a small torch in the dark forest. It doesn't show everything at once, but gives enough light for the next step to be safe. You have been cheated by your life, and I'm cheated by my own feelings. What we both need is friendship. Will you be my best friend?
Happy Birthday —

A…N…N…A…V…I

Yes!' she said and hugged him.
☺

SURPRISE #13
1:00 pm
(13th hour of surprise)

Harshil plugged the head-phones and told her to listen. Now what's this?' she asked
Just keep calm and listen.
Harshil tuned the local FM radio station, and Annavi was extremely happy when the famous Radio Jockey of the city wished her on air. Lucky girl!
☺

SURPRISE #14
2:00 pm
(14th hour of surprise)

Bunny was right when he suggested that each and every

relationship begins with friendship. In order to strengthen this friendship, Harshil took her at the place she had never been before.

You're a rich person. You will always prefer to go to expensive hotels for food, but today, I'll make you feel like a normal middle class girl,'

Though Annavi managed to smile, she felt uncomfortable on seeing the untidy sight of the street food.

Don't you think this place is little dirty?' she said.

But the food is very tasty,' replied Harshil.

From boiled noodles to the spicy ones — such was her transformation that day.

SURPRISE #15
3:00 pm
(16th hour of surprise)

It's good to shed tears for the one who is ready to wipe them off at the very next second.

The street food was bit spicy for Annavi to resist. Water flooded out from her eyes, but Harshil was there to make it up for her.

After so many years, Annavi was nostalgic about her childhood. Although she was smiling, the bunch cotton candies were flashing the sweet memories of her past.

SURPRISE #16
4:00 pm
(16th hour of surprise)

Do you see that wedding procession?' Harshil
asked. Yes, all are dancing and enjoying in that
Baraat,' He held her hand and said, Come, let's go,'

No way,' she said. I can't dance on the street like
that,'

Before she could deny, Harshil forcefully dragged her
into the *Baraat*. How to dance?' she screamed, owing to the
loud music of orchestra.

This is a free platform. The way you wish, you can
dance.' he shouted.

If that is the case, let the music rock.' she said and
danced like there was no tomorrow. Yes. She was happy.

☺

SURPRISE #17

17:00 pm

(17th hour of surprise)

What can I assume?' she asked him. He didn't reply.

You're taking me to your house like that. What can I
assume?' she asked again.

Nothing.' Harshil said. Annavi was little puzzled.

Annavi, this is my Mom's room. Come inside,' he
said.

Annavi came inside and sat on the chair which was kept near
the wardrobe. Harshil opened the wardrobe and took out
four sets of red bangles. He then gave those bangles to her
and said, After my Father's demise, my Mother never looked
at these bangles. Maybe it was due to the fear of our society.
But then, I forced her to wear it because I wanted her to see
and love all the colors. No person in this world is only
limited to black or white color. Today, I'm giving this

148

to you, because I also want you to live a colorful life. Happy Birthday, Annavi.'

☺

SURPRISE #18
6:00 pm
(18th hour of surprise)

Which girl on the earth doesn't want to feel special on her birthday? The feeling that was running through Annavi's mind was indescribable. No guy had ever done so much for her. She knew that she was falling for him.

Not only did he make feel special, but after so many years she felt alive. And once if any girl feels alive because of some guy, then she falls in love with him.

Can I ask you something?' she asked him.

Not now. After few minutes,' he replied as he was preparing himself for her 18th surprise.

It's important,'

Tell.'

Why are you doing all this?' she asked him suddenly. Is it necessary to tell the reason?'

Yes it is,' she said. I mean, how could you do all this? How could you make each and every hour of this day special?' she asked.

Just like that,' Harshil replied.

Like what?'

Turn around; you'll get your answer,' he said.

She turned around and saw her image in the mirror. A short message was written on it with the red lipstick—*I wish I were this mirror. At least I would have lived your image and thus conclude that all the girls are not the same. Happy*

Birthday – A... N... N... A... V... I

☺

SURPRISE #19
7:00 pm
(19th hour of surprise)

It was like a dream come true for Annavi. Although he was writing her name in some or the other form in all the surprise, she felt as if he was rewriting the new form of her personality upon her heart.

I'm feeling so happy,' she said.
The person who has never seen much happiness in his life always makes others happy and Harshil was doing the same for Annavi. He took her inside the kitchen and cooked something for her.

When a guy makes food, it's always full of flaws. The food was awful; still Annavi feasted it with a big smile on her face.

Harshil had so much of respect for her; likewise, Annavi had the same respect to appreciate his every effort. Eventually when Harshil tasted the same food, he apologized for having spoiled that surprise for her. Annavi kissed his chin and the answer was clear –
If in any relationship when efforts are appreciated then there is no space for expectations.

☺

SURPRISE #20
8 :00 pm
(20th hour of surprise)

Can I ask for one surprise?'

Harshil nodded.

I've not slept. I'm feeling little sleepy,' she said.

Sure. You can sleep inside my Mom's bedroom,' he said.

I said that I want a surprise. Can you accompany me?' she said.

This time I'm not in a hangover,'

I ensure nothing will happen. I just want to hug you and sleep,'

But Annavi…'

Please, Harshil. It's my birthday. And this is the only surprise I'm asking for,'

Her innocence was adequate to convince him.
She encircled her arms over him and said, I'm exhausted. I can't walk. Can you help me?'

Harshil grabbed her back and then he lifted her in his wings and took her inside the bedroom. He placed her on the bed. She refrained to separate her hands from his neck. She intentionally pulled him and as a result, their lips had a soft touch. She closed her eyes and invoked a tender moan. Harshil stayed there and cuddled Annavi upfront.
He was playing with her glossy hair. He said, Open up your eyes, Annavi. The moments that we experience with our open eyes are always real,'

Annavi didn't open her eyes. By this mere action, she recreated the concrete meaning of trust. Both of them had kept each other's word of not fitting in a move further, but they felt they were badly stuck in between.
Excited hormones were just driving her to kiss him, while the same excited hormones were also provoking the man of the hour to kiss her. Eventually, he got a strong hold over

his feelings.

Harshil rubbed his thumb over her soft lips. He undid her eyes and said, Actually my next surprise is here itself in this bedroom,'

He got up and bent down to pop something beneath the bed. When Annavi found him motionless for minutes, she herself turned down and inquired, What are you doing?'

I'm shaking,' he said in a mischievous tone.

Shaking what?'

Can't you guess?'

She laughed and said, Oh Fuck! Is this a place to masturbate?'

Immediately Harshil came out and opened the knob of the champagne bottle. He altered the bottle's opening towards Annavi and said, I was shaking this!'

As he cut off his thumb from the bottle's knob, the champagne ruptured out and wetted Annavi so hard that she remained quiet for scant flashes.

Harshil laughed and said, Happy Birthday Annavi,' Annavi chased him until she emptied the remaining champagne over his scalp.

☺

SURPRISE #21
9:00 pm
(21st hour of surprise)

This is my final surprise, Annavi.' he said.

Why final? Still three hours are left,'

True, but I've no right on those three hours,'

What are you saying? If this whole day belonged to you, then why not these three hours?'

They are meant for someone very special,' She was puzzled.

Take out your cell phone, Annavi.' Why?'

Do as I say.'

She took out her cell phone.

Now?' she asked.

Harshil went near her and said in a muffled tone, Call your parents,'

Annavi blew up with a shout, Have you gone mad? Do you have any idea of what you're telling?'

Stop shouting!'

You're forcing me. You know nothing,' she said. Annavi...'

Shut up! I hate them. Do you hear that? I hate them,'

She added, 'Not only because I'm their daughter, but I hate them for being my parents.'

Why do you have so much of animosity for them?' My

day was so awesome,' she said. But at this hour, you're spoiling my mood,'

Harshil grabbed her hands and took her to the window and asked, Do you see this sky?' Annavi nodded.

As a boy, when I asked about my Dad, Mother used to say that my Dad was so great that he didn't live with us. He lived in the sky along with other stars. So I used to stand at this same window and gazed to discover that one star which belonged to my Father,' He took a pause and said, And do you know Annavi, till this date I'm finding that star,'

Annavi showed no reaction. He shrugged her shoulders

and said, You cannot unite with someone after they leave this place. Mistakes are done by everyone, Annavi, but that doesn't imply we should hate them for rest of your life. As you're mounting up with success, don't you see they are growing old?'

They need you Annavi,' he remarked.

But they never made an attempt to contact me,' She said.

They must be feeling sorry about their act. Don't make them suffer more from this guilt. Today is your birthday — the day on which they brought you into this world. Can't this be the same day when they will again get their daughter back?'

They never loved me!'

They love you, Annavi,' he said. Call them,' he appealed.

No. They will talk rudely,'

If they talk rudely, I promise that I'll never tell you to call them again. But just now, give a shot,'

Her hands shivered as she typed the phone number on the screen. She stayed for a while and looked at him. Harshil blinked his sights to ease her and thus she swiped her thumb to make a call.

EVERYONE WILL GET THE ANSWER

Annavi's Father picked up the call. She turned red out of fear.

Annavi: Hello, papa?

                        There was a brief silence.

Father: Who is this?

Annavi: You hate me so much that you can't even recognize my voice?

Father: Annaviiiii….

Annavi: Hmmm

Father: Yes, Madam.

Annavi: From where do you bring so much of hatred for me?

Father: I don't have your mobile number, but I frequently call you on your office number.

Annavi: Why do you do that?

Father: With a hope that someday you will accidentally pick up my call, I will hear your voice, and then cut the call.

Annavi: But you never came to meet me.

Father: Madam, I daily see you. You're a big person now, so you only look at the people of your status.

Annavi: Why are you constantly addressing me as Madam'? And when did you see me?

Father: You're my Madam because you pay me. And I
             see you daily because I'm the security guard of
             your office.

Annavi got the biggest shock of her life. She dragged her
palm over her lips and hesitantly opened the pdf list of all
the people working in her office. Somewhere in between
she saw her Father's name. She sat down and cried like a
baby.

Annavi: I'm sorry, papa.
Father: No, Annavi. We are sorry. We treated you….
Annavi: I miss you and Mumma at every second of
             my life.
Father: Your Mumma misses you more than I do.
             You know, today she has prepared a
             sweet dish because it's you birthday.
             Happy birthday, Annavi.
Annavi: Why are you working as a security guard?
Father: Just for your smile. To see it every day and tell
             you Mother that her Girl has all grown up to
             become a successful business woman.

Annavi was in no state to hear anything further. She cut
the call and smacked her cell phone. She cried until she
felt diminished. Harshil hugged her and said, I told
you.cSee they love you,'
    I love you,' she said giving him a tight hug.
Harshil wiped off her tears but even his eyes were moist.
    Now go, and complete your family,' he said.
    Will you accompany me?'
    Not today!' he responded.

How will I face them alone?'

You never have to face your own parents. You only have to hug them.'

Annavi smiled and said, That accidental intimacy with you was the best thing that ever happened to me,' She thanked Harshil for everything, and left to embrace the last surprise of the day.

☺

After Annavi had left the place, Harshil opened the cupboard and took out the urn which had the ashes of his Mother. He kissed the urn because he learned that somewhere in every girl there was a part of his Mother. Bunny, who calmly watched everything came in and said, You should now dissolve these ashes in the river,'

They followed all the rituals and went to river Yumana. Bunny said, Go and make her free from all the bonds of this world,'

Harshil held Bunny's hand and said, You're my brother, so you're also her son. Come. Together we shall do this,'

Both of them submerged half inside the river. Harshil opened the urn and touched those ashes for the one last time. This time there were no tears in his eyes because he felt that "the forever smile" of his Mother would stay there with him for rest of his life. Slowly and gradually, Bunny and Harshil inverted the urn, and dissolved those ashes in the holy river, Yamuna.

☺

Life's set, Harshil. Why don't you marry Annavi?' Bunny asked.

Let her live. Just a few moments back, she has got her family. And you want me to take it away from her by asking her to marry me?'

Strike when the iron is hot. Haven't you heard this saying? This is an exact stage to propose her,'

Okay, I've an idea,' Harshil said. Do one thing. Book a huge hall and invite each and every one from her office for the dinner. Arrange two rings and a stage. If she agrees, I'll tie the knot there itself. If she denies, then well, we will just enjoy the dinner and return,' he added.

Now that's a nice idea!' Bunny exclaimed. Don't you want to sleep? You've not slept since last twenty-four hours,'

It feels like I was sleeping for years,' Harshil responded.

Even after a person dies, the blood inside the body keeps fluctuating for a while. Same way, when one person leaves another one under the pretext of love, the memories keep fluctuating.

Manshita had left him at the time he needed the most. He concluded that no relationship could survive without an essence of friendship. Harshil loved Manshita and Manshita liked Harshil, but they were never great friends. Had they been perfect friends, things would have been totally different!

Like any normal person, Harshil had full rights to hate Manshita for what she had done to him but had she not left him, he would have not come across a sweet person as Annavi.

Manshita had broken his trust. Despite of that fact, he didn't hate her because he understood that she was never worth of his trust. Harshil could never forget her because every single time when he glanced at the mirror, he regretted of not being as serene as other dudes were. And then one fine day, she entered his life; he saw his image in her eyes and realized that he was special.

A person who wants a commitment is a person who wants to live life. While others, only survive by sharing their feelings at the randomness of attraction.

It was as simple as that. Harshil wanted a commitment and he expected Manshita to be like him. At the other hand, Manshita acted according to the situation. Both of them were right in their own ways. They were just not right about each other.

She had a heart.
He too had a heart
Then why did they fear to beat together?

They loved each other.
They cared for each other.
Then why did they fear from accepting each other?

That midnight was the most important one for Annavi. Harshil wanted to call her. He gazed at her number, but later on dropped the idea as he wanted her to enjoy that moment with her family.

☺

The next day…

Harshil. Get up fast,' Bunny
shouted What wrong?' he asked.

He dragged Harshil to the drawing room and said, I can't understand this news…'

Harshil looked over the news showing exclusively that the leading business tycoon of Delhi, Annavi Datta had committed suicide, the preceding midnight.

Harshil?'

Bunny, this is someone else. Annavi is a strong woman. She got her family. She has no reason in her life to take such a step,'
Bunny was motionless.

Hey, it's not our Annavi yaar,' Harshil said positively.

Harshil, I made a call to her office. They have confirmed me about the same,'

Harshil was inflamed. He tried to call Annavi, but it showed out of coverage. Okay, come let's go and check. I know her, she is very strong. She will never end her life like this!'

After a long search, both of them found Annavi's actual house, where she used to stay with her family in past. A huge crowd had assembled outside that house. Observing so, Harshil felt uneasy.

Bunny inquired from one guy who said that last night three people had committed suicide inside that house.

Police drove the crowd away. People from the ambulance rushed inside and brought those three dead bodies out from the house. Bunny protected Harshil because he knew that something very uncertain was on its way. Coincidently, Harshil saw the same the Policemen who had released him on Annavi's request.

Harshil rushed towards him and said, Sir…'

What are you doing here?' Policemen asked.

Is Annavi dead?' he asked.

Policemen removed his hat. He was speechless.

Is she dead?' Harshil asked as tears railed down from his eyes.

The Policemen said, Come. Sit inside my van. We will discuss everything at the Police Station.'

☺

At the Police Station

You've not answered my question, sir. Is she dead?'

It's tough to believe that a strong business lady like her would take such a step. Yes, she is no more. Last night, she had committed suicide along with her Parents,'

One statement broke his heart forever. What had not taken place in his life? It all started from his Mother's death, followed by Manshita's exit, and now this suicide incident.

The Policemen broke the silence as he said, It's a pure case of suicide. In the postmortem reports we discovered no traces of murder,'

Why did she do so?' Bunny asked.

Every answer to your question is hidden in these suicide notes. And one more thing—I was always faithful to Annavi madam. She has clearly written two important things in her last note,' he said.

What did she write?' Bunny asked.

She has appealed not to release these notes in public, and second, she has clearly written that only Harshil can only read these notes,'

Thank you so much, Mr. Ali.' Bunny said as he read the Policemen's name from his batch.

Mr. Ali handed over those suicide notes to Harshil. He took the notes and silently went to one corner to read. After a few minutes he came back and sat on the same chair. He refrained from making an eye contact with anyone.

Bunny looked at him and said, I'm going to cancel the hall that we had hired for this evening,'

No, don't cancel. Let the things happen as they were planned,'

No one will come,' Bunny said. You know, people are saying random things under your name. As you were close to Annavi, they are blaming you for all this,'

Mr. Ali interrupted and said, He is right. It will be a wise step if you stay away from public, at least for a few months,'

Bunny, don't cancel anything. This evening should go ahead as per the plans,'

But Harshil….'

Shut up! Do as I say. I'm the boss,' Harshil responded rudely.

Boss?'

That's correct. He is rightfully an owner of Annavi's multinational company,' said Mr. Ali. She has legally given her every property and shares to Harshil,'

How is this possible?' Bunny asked

See, these are the original documents. Now everything belongs to Harshil,'

Bunny desperately wanted to read those suicide notes but he knew he had to respect Annavi's wish.

One more thing,' Mr. Ali added. Her brothers are not ready to accept the responsibility for her funeral. They don't consider her as their sister. So, in that case, government will claim the right on her dead body. If you guys are ready to take the responsibility of her funeral, I can hand over her body to you,' Mr. Ali said.

Harshil agreed to take the responsibility and requested Mr. Ali to not let media know anything about her funeral.

Mr. Ali arranged one quiet location away from the city for her funeral. After following all the rituals, Harshil offered fire to Annavi's body.

Bunny's eyes were damp, but there wasn't a single drop of tear in Harshil's eyes. Rather, those fire flames were giving him some sort of energy.

Life is so uncertain. Before twenty-four hours, he was giving her surprises, and now, she was converted to ashes. When her remains cooled down, he collected them in an earthen pot. After that, he didn't look back. He walked off because he knew that turning back would result into a serious downpour.

Have you invited everyone for the evening?' Harshil asked Bunny.

Brother, they will kill you,'

You cannot kill someone who is already dead,'

I can't understand. What has she written in those notes? And why did she give you her whole company?'

Make sure that you invited everyone from her office. This evening, everyone will get the answer,'

☺   ☺   ☺

WHERE MONEY CAN BUY HAPPINESS

It was going to be the toughest walk for Harshil. Much tougher than the one which he took for Manshita when he entered in IIT to get the job.

The people working in Annavi's office were shocked and saddened due to her dead. Various speculations were being made regarding her suicide, and some of the employees had an eye on Harshil as he was the only one close to her in those last days.

As expected, all the employees came to the hall. Harshil came inside and went on the stage. Bunny stood right in front of him so that he could save Harshil if anyone physically abused him.

Good evening everyone,' he said and greeted them with a smile.
No one greeted him back. Instead, everyone gave him a fierce glance.

Well, I know that some of you might have opened the recording application from your smart phones,' he said.

You guys want to record whatever I say and then give to the press, isn't it?'

One of the senior most employees from the group responded, Yes. We loved our madam. You don't know what you've taken apart from us,'

If you think that I'm the reason your madam is not there in this world, then you are free to lodge a doubt against me,' Harshil said.

Now you've the power. You can do anything,'

Sir, I'm standing right in front of you. There is no backup, and you guys are in group,'

He added, I've invited you all because I want to say something, and after that, you can do whatever you want!'

He took out those suicide notes from his blazer and said, You might have seen in the news that there were no suicide notes, but the reality is different. Before I quote whatever is written in these two suicide notes; I would like to tell you all about us....'

Harshil narrated every single thing about him and Annavi. Most of the ladies from the group had tears in their eyes when they heard about those special surprises for Annavi on her birthday.

So now, since you know everything about us, I'll first read the suicide written by her Parents...'

Dear Annavi,

We are sorry for treating you the way you never deserved.

Do you remember that day when you proclaimed that one day you would make us feel proud?

I and your Mother always considered that girls were the fragile elements of our society. We wanted to lock you inside the house and undertake your marriage as soon as possible because we wanted to sustain our respect in the society. But you proved us wrong.

You proved that respect of any family is not only limited to the society, but it's also related to their daughter's wish. We always saved money for your marriage — may be just to feed this hungry society on that day, but we never thought of saving it for your further studies.

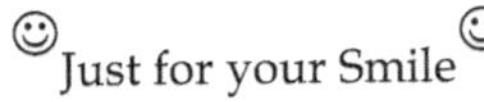
Just for your Smile   Baman Tadiwala

*You made us realize that true investment of any family should
be for the education of their daughter, and not for her one-day
marriage ceremony.*

Yes, we had tortured you.

*It's true, we loved your brothers more than we ever loved you
and trust me, we have paid the price for the same.*

We offered them everything, and they left us for nothing.

*Sorry — is a very small word to say, but my daughter, we're
really very sorry. We love you, and we wish we could stay with
you. But there is always a punishment for crime. So today, I and
your Mother are punishing each other for the endless sufferings
that we gave you.*

*You don't know this, but we had committed a grave crime in
past. In past when you had left our house, due to the fear of
society, we had ordered your brothers to finish you.*

*Today we are finishing ourselves because we both won't be able
to face you and look into your eyes and say — Wish you were
our only child!*

And now, I'm reading Annavi's suicide note...'

Respected Reader,

Will you grant my two last wishes?

First wish: You will not leak this letter in front of media.

Second wish: You will give this letter to Harshil.

*Whatever I'm writing below is for him, and for my adorable
staff. Harshil,*

*I'm writing this letter as a third person because I have no guts
to speak. Never hate your Annavi for this. It was because of you,
she lived those twenty-four hours of her birthday like twenty-
four lives. You know, every guy she met only wanted to touch
her body, but you were the only one who touched her heart.*

166

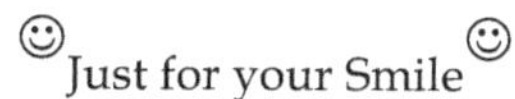

Just for your Smile   Baman Tadiwala

You made her feel special like no guy had ever done. And most importantly, you were the reason she got her parents back.

But who gave them the right to go away like this? Annavi was correct when she told you that they don't love her. If they loved her, then they would have never left her like this.

Now, she needs to find an answer. Therefore, she is also choosing the same way. Guilt is a bitch. It not only kills you from inside, but it also finishes you forever. Annavi's guilt is forcing her to go on the same way.

Harshil, just remember — Annavi loves you, and she will always be there with you. It's just that now she cannot survive because her parents had to die as she was the reason of their guilt.

Annavi has proved herself. She has earned millions. She had always dominated people by the power of her money, but today, same money looks powerless as it cannot bring her parents back.

She is officially giving you her wealth. You're now an owner of this company which she had created on her own.

You always loved your Mother. You loved a girl, and for her, you entered IIT to give an interview for the job. This way you met Annavi. She liked you, and rest is the history. You know, she trusts you more than she loves you. So she believes you'll never misuse her wealth.

Take this company to a next level. At such a level from where it will follow your own motto? Don't you know that motto? It is —
JUST FOR YOUR SMILE.

You always did special things for your Mother, Annavi, and Manshita, so now it's time to do something — just for your smile!

Annavi wishes you to change the mindset of the society. Annavi wishes you to work hard for her company and generate enough money to help the ones who really need it because sometimes, money can definitely buy happiness — in the form someone's smile. That's all she wants from you. Will you fulfill her last wish, Harshil?

And To my dear staff,

I know, this moment is very tough for all of us. But I promise if you all support Harshil and continue to work with the same spirit, then he will never disappoint you. Just show him little love, and he will never leave you.

You see...if a person like me could feel special with him, then you guys are totally a special thing. I've never jotted my decision on anyone, so today also I'll not force you. But if see a trace of love and respect for me in his eyes, then please support him. Harshil,

Now Annavi is going, but she has seen a big dream today.

In her dream, the song of hope is playing. This song is giving her an essence of life and love. She knows that a person who commits suicide never rests in peace. She will come back. May be in the worst condition, but then she will be happy to see you as a millionaire.

Annavi loves you, and now she is leaving.

☺

There was a brief silence in the entire hall for a few minutes. The same employee who had initially blamed Harshil came forward and started applauding. Seeing them, all the other employees also applauded. Bunny was not able to control his tears, he too joined the applause.

We are so sorry, sir. We weren't aware about this. Annavi madam was everything to us, and now you're everything to us,'

You're older than me, sir. Please don't address me as sir. You can call me by my name,' Harshil said politely. This time the ladies came forward, and the one of them said, We definitely see that love and respect in your eyes. We see that dedication for Annavi madam in your heart.

And most importantly, we also see the respect for all of us in your behavior. So fearlessly you expressed your feelings in front of us without even caring about our reaction! You know sir, Annavi madam was also fearless. We don't know about anyone, but we are all with you,'

Slowly and gradually, all of them agreed to support him. They came and stood alongside him on the stage. Only Bunny was left on the other side.

Don't you wish to join?' Harshil asked him.

I don't have much knowledge about the business, sir. Even if you give me the job as a sweeper in your office, I'll happily do it. Can I join?'

Harshil smiled and opened his arms and said, This is not my office, it's our office.'

☺

Harshil now had the solid purpose to work in his life. From the very next day, he started working hard. He decided to make each and every day count and vowed to fulfill Annavi's wish. *When a leader leads from the front, whole team is inspired to work hard.*

Harshil showed his dedication like no one ever did. He used to set the target on one paper and worked until it wasn't accomplished. For several months, he didn't go his home to sleep. At night, when he felt exhausted, he slept on the office floor, and again woke up early in the morning to work for that target.

Seeing this heat of passion inside his heart, each and every member of his staff became regular. After one and a half year, Annavi's company took a forward gear. It made a tremendous rise in terms of profits. Local newspapers and media noticed this thing, and narrated it in positive way across the entire state.

Slowly after two more years, Annavi's company became one of the fastest growing companies of India. By that time, Harshil had discovered a hidden talent inside Bunny. He saw that his friend was an excellent orator, and had great management skills. Therefore, he took a bold decision and made him CEO of the company.

Initially a few people were against this decision, but Bunny proved everyone wrong. He traveled across entire India for an year and increased the shareholders for Annavi's company.

In no time, the company started gaining international attention. Few big multinational foreign companies decided to merge with Annavi's company, and the profits continued to flourish. After earning tremendous profit, Harshil thought of utilizing that money for fulfilling Annavi's wish. As per her wish, he had spent that money to help the one who really needed it.

—*There should be no second Annavi in this world, who would give up her life because of some guilt.*‖—This was his vision.

Each and every person has at least one moment which he can cherish as a golden phase in his life. The golden phase of the company began when it grounded its subsidiary branch in London. The profits obtained from there were utilized for the operation cost of women who suffered from the breast cancer.

Harshil decided that the company should also have some subtitle under its name. After hearing numerous suggestions, he created a new brand under the name of –

ANNAVI

          ……….where money can buy happiness
                    ☺   ☺   ☺

BACK IN THE PRESENT

And with that the press conference also ended. All the reporters who were initially against Harshil stood up, and applauded him out of respect.

Bunny looked at Amayraj and said, And you are creating a story out of such a noble person who is a silent messiah for so many unfortunates?'

Amayraj looked at Harshil. He was embarrassed and he didn't know what to say. He got up from his place and this time he asked Harshil in a very polite tone, You've still not answered my question, sir. Why are you still unmarried?'

Harshil gave a smile and said, Personally, it's my destiny. I loved my Mother, and she left me. I loved Manshita, and she also left. Finally, when I started to love Annavi, she decided to end her life. Love is not made for me,'

Didn't you have any personal dream after that incident?'

My each and every dream died on the day she left all of us like that. Of course, I love her, but I'll never forgive her for the way she left. Suicide is never a solution of any problem. It's just a way to escape. Sometimes I think what if I had gone along with her that day to meet her Parents?'

Then she would be still there with all of us,' Amayraj said and wiped his eyes.

Harshil giggled and said, You see, it was meant to happen. It was a pure destiny of our love story!'

One last question before I promise not broadcast this press conference on any news channel,' Amayraj said.

Thank you. I'm glad you understood and maintained your promise, as well as mine!'

Will you forgive me for my act?' and as Amayraj said so, he fell down on his knees.

Harshil lifted him up and embraced him saying, It's okay,'

I'm guilty. I just wanted to earn little bit of popularity so I wrote a fake love story under your name. Please forgive me,' Amayraj said.

You're still very young, Amayraj. When I was of your age, I also made one mistake when I entered IIT illegally, and you know what followed after that.

I want you to learn to respect your job,' he said. Media is *for* the people and *by* the people, but it's never *of* the people. It's totally of the reporters and journalists like you, and everyone else inside this room. The mass only believes whatever you guys present in front of them. And don't be guilty, I was never really enraged,' Harshil added.

Amayraj then took the camera from the camera man, and dropped it on the floor. This indicated that whatever was conversed inside would stay secret between them.

☺

After one year
2018

Amayraj revisited Harshil again. Not for an interview this time, but for something else.

I don't see your articles in newspapers these days. Is everything alright?' Harshil asked.

Amayraj smiled and said, It's been so long since I left

journalism,'

Why?'

That's because of you,'

Oh! I'm sorry,'

No. Accidentally, it was the best thing that ever happened to me.'

How?' Harshil asked.

He handed over the marriage invitation card and said, I tried different things in my life, and while exploring; I found someone of my type.'

On seeing that marriage invitation card, Harshil became extremely happy and congratulated Amayraj.

So you have to come to attend my

marriage,' For sure,'

And everyone from ANNAVI are also invited,' Amayraj added.

Everyone will surely come,'

Amayraj looked at Bunny and said, Bunny bhai, please *kaha suna sab maaf!* Do come.'

Bunny congratulated Amayraj and said, We have all moved on from the old Amayraj. This one is really cool by the way,'

Actually I need one help from you guys,' Amayraj said.

What sort of help?' Bunny asked.

We all are so similar,' he said. I was an orphan, and I still remember there was one lady, who always did something special for me. Since you at ANNAVI, honor such people, I will be awesome if you can felicitate this lady as well,'

Of course, we will honor her. What is her name?' Bunny asked.

Well, I don't know her name,'

Do you have her address or something?'

No, I've nothing. I just have her photo. You people have great contacts. I'm sure, you'll find her,'

Amayraj gave one envelope to Hashil and said, That's it. If possible, please help me. I will be really happy,'

After giving that envelope to Harshil, Amayraj immediately left the cabin.

He is strange!' Bunny exclaimed.

Harshil opened that envelope. Actually, it was a sketch.

I mean, what is this? I've seen someone like her,' Bunny said as his eyes got stuck to that sketch. Even Harshil was equally stunned.

Don't you think we have seen someone like her?' Bunny asked.

Tears feel down from Harshil's eyes.

Hey, what happened?' Bunny

asked. This face, Bunny,'

What are you saying?'

This is Manshita,' Harshil silently whispered.

☺

This meant that Amayraj was the same guy, who as a kid, always followed Harshil and Manshita whenever they met. He now realized the purpose of that sketch book, and a pencil in the hands of that small kid.

Bunny immediately rushed out of the cabin to stop Amayraj. He was quietly standing outside the cabin with pity face.

You were right about everything, Bunny bhai. But Manshita di never misused the money which she took from Harshil,' Amayraj said. At present you're working for everyone's smile, but years ago she did the same for unfortunates like me.' he added.

Amayraj looked at Harshil and said, You boycotted her for years. You lived on her smile, but you didn't even realize the purpose of those yellow smile balls?' Harshil just laughed at his destiny.

How is she?'

She is also coming to my wedding,'

Is she happy with her husband?' Harshil asked as her happiness still mattered a lot to him.

Do you really think that she was serious about Hridant?'

Yes,'

Amayraj smiled and replied, At one stage, your Mother wanted you to leave Manshita, but you didn't leave her because you loved her. Then after Mrs. Rama passed away, Manshita di thought of completing her wish. So, she had to lie,'

Harshil turned blue out of guilt. He controlled those tears and looked at the other way around instead of making an eye contact with Amayraj.

You were the last guy in her life!' Amayraj said and left the office.

EPILOGUE

Amayraj's wedding day

The moment finally arrived when Harshil saw Manshita after so many years. He envisioned that scenario when he saw her for the very first on the bullet. At present, she was busy in beautifying the bride.
When she was about to apply the eyeliner, Harshil interrupted and said, No not this!'

Manshita stopped. Eyeliner pencil fell down when she heard that familiar voice. She looked up, and found Harshil right in front of her. It was like a dream for her.

I mean to say...Every ordinary eye looks extra ordinary when you apply eyeliner,'

Manshita just smiled and responded, You're still a fan of these pencils?'

What to do? Many a times I tried to erase it from my life, but as you know, these eyeliners are waterproofed. They don't go so easily.'

I've heard a lot about ANNAVI. You're seriously doing a great job for the people,' she said.

Thank you!' he said. I hope that you and Hridant are living happily?'

Yeah, we are living happily,' she replied.

And what about the babies?'

We have not planned. Let

see,' Wow! I mean just wow!'

She laughed and asked, For what?'

For hiding your tears so skillfully,' he said. And for so skillfully producing this fake smile,'

I don't know what to say,' she said.

That's actually a nice way to escape. The way you always did, but not today,'

I have only brought problems in your life. We are not meant for each other,' she said.

You will not decide everything. Even I don't want you. You left me at the time when I needed you the most,'

I'm sorry. I did this because......'

There is no space for because today,' shouted Amayraj from behind. Di, will you excuse us for a minute?' he said holding Harshil's hand.

No, I hate this. Whatever you want to say, say it in front of me,'

Okay then, listen. My wife's family is very religious. They have specially invited this royal Panditji from Varanasi. He was brought under the promise to carry out two marriage ceremonies,'

What's the problem in that?' Manshita asked.

He says that he won't leave this place unless and until he completes two marriage ceremonies. Now, from where will I get a second fresh couple?'

Give him double the amount of money, and tell him to F***,' said vintage Manshita.

He is stubborn. He won't leave like that,' Amayraj said.

So what do you want me to do in this matter?' she shouted aloud. Do you want me to sit in this Mandap?'

Yeah, that's actually a nice idea,' Harshil said. If you don't mind, I can accompany you.'

Di, what are you thinking? My marriage is in danger!'
Okay. Let's give a shot.' Manshita submitted.

☺   ☺   ☺

9 789353 519827